Private Message

Danielle Torella

Interior Design by Angela McLaurin, Fictional Formats

Cover Photo taken by David Massa

Cover Models: Joe Marvullo & Sam Roman

Cover designer: Randy Potvin

Table of Contents

Dedication

To anyone who has been told they can't.

Chapter One

Tess

At the end of last week's drawing lesson, Ms. Sawyer, my middle-aged hippie-chick art instructor, informed us that we would have a male model to observe and paint for tonight's class. I never gave it a second thought beyond *God I hope it's someone remotely attractive after last week's lesson of trees. Like seriously, trees?*

As always, I am the last to arrive. But, hey, this time it wasn't my fault. I swear my car keys had more of a social life than me and had a fling with the sneaker I couldn't find while getting I was getting ready. Rushing into class, I assumed my usual position in the corner table away from "the action," as Ms. S liked to put it. I flip past last week's assignment to an open page. *God I can't draw a tree to save my life...*

I look to my right to see another student halfway through his drawing, scanning from the top of his pad down to the bottom, and that's when I notice the subject. I snap my head up so rapidly I think I got whiplash. He's sitting perfectly still on top of a table, his back to me, thank God, because I realize that my mouth is hanging open. Ms. S clears her throat and I glance at her, as she waves her hand in the direction of the model and forms her hand to look like she's hold a pencil and drawing... *yeah yeah I'm getting to work.*

I take in his midnight dark short hair, casually styled as a faux hawk, then I scan to his neck, down to his toned shoulders, which adorn a collection of black and gray tattoo work, but I can't make out the detail. Man, I should have gotten my shit together and got to class on time. Then maybe I could have grabbed a seat a little closer. One of his arms is bent and appears to be holding him up. His right leg is bent and I can only assume the other is out in front of himself but stupid me—being late, I got stuck only looking at his back straight on...*so much for interesting...*

I begin to sketch, and by the time I get down to the lowest part of his back, I find myself biting my bottom lip and just staring. *Come on, Tess, get your crap together if you want to finish the assignment!*

"All right, everyone, class is dismissed. Next week we will continue with our model here," Ms. Sawyer announces, while winking in the direction of the beautiful creature up on display, and obviously before I can even finish. Damn *shame too...*

"Tess, a moment please, after you clean up," she says as I pack up. I look back up to the table for a quick look at the face of the back, but I get only a quick profile look and notice his sleek black leather jacket that hugs his slender frame. *Total damn shame...*

"Tess, you have been late the last four classes, and you haven't completed a full drawing for two weeks. What is going on?" Ms. S gives me a sympathetic look, but her tone makes me feel like a child.

"I am sorry, Ms. Sawyer," I tell her. "I have been working the afternoon shift and the coffee shop filled up after classes let out and I couldn't leave." I want to add that I had requested countless times to be switched to the morning shift, but I don't.

"If you want to pass my class, you best be on time from now on. You're talented, Tess. Don't flush it down the drain." She is a strict professor but compassionate and passionate when it comes to art. I guess I should respect that and make a better effort.

Drawing, painting and photography mean the absolute world to me. Art grounds me. It makes me feel. I had plans after high school to get into art school, but lost hope over time, ever since my high school art teacher gave me crap about not letting her touch my painting, because she knew what looked "right." I wasn't going to let her change my piece like so many of the other students did. Yeah, one student allowed her to all the time, and eventually she gave him a great reference letter to a famous art academy in New York City...*yeah great.*

And on top of that, my dad was never supportive, always telling me, "Art isn't a future. Art doesn't make the money. Art isn't a LIFE." I shut down after that point. Granted, my mom was behind me, but it's always been just me and her. She's the cool understanding mom. She made me want to stay home on weekends while the other kids were at parties or sporting events. I liked being home; my mom was and still sort of is my best friend. But as much as I love her, I needed to be out on my own. I was too shy and reliant on others to do things for me, because I wasn't comfortable with it. So I took the initiative to get a job and move out, even if that means struggling.

So my crappy grades got even worse, and I barely got my high school diploma. So here I am at a community college attempting to pay for what few classes I can afford on the double shifts I tend to fill at the coffee shop. I'll do anything to be able to let my creative juices flow.

"Yes ma'am" was all I said, and then I scurried out of the classroom.

In crisp fall night air, on my way to my car, I let out a huge sigh. Holy crap, that guy was hot! Well, I think he was, I did only get to see his back after all *and what a back it was...*

Yeah, I need a drink, a big one, and I'm not usually a drinker. Christ, it takes me over a week to get through a bottle of my favorite cheap wine, and I know I only have less than half a bottle sitting in my fridge. That surely won't be enough to take the edge off.

What is wrong with me? I see a freaking man's back and I'm all tight and my stomach is twisted...in THAT way. God, I've never even had sex before and all I can think about is digging my nails into that man's back! And that's a first considering what happened that one night three years ago when I went to a concert alone. I never wanted or considered a man laying a hand on me...until now. I need a bar. I never go to a bar, but after tonight I think it calls for some rum!

Driving through the streets of Seattle on my way home, I look left and right in search for basic bar to just chill out and unwind. *Yeah, like you won't still think about the fine male specimen you were oh so lucky to stare at only twenty minutes ago!* Ah, here we go. I pull into the parking lot of the modest brick building with a dark green awning, check my face in my rearview mirror. It's about as good as it going to get, but hey, I wouldn't be here if I wasn't feeling so rough, and I can only assume it shows.

Inside, I am flooded with the smooth voice of Adam Levine singing about being sad, and I take a seat at the bar.

I order a rum and coke. The burly-looking bartender cards me.

He looks like a human teddy bear in a plaid shirt.

As he makes my drink, I glance down and notice the bar's name on a beer list in one of those clear stand-up displays:

"Welcome to Chatz. Log in. Let your inhibitions run wild."

What the hell does that mean? Before I can continue reading, a young woman plops down on the stool next to me. She's at least half a foot taller than me, with long soft red hair, and a form-fitting emerald green dress. She nods at the display.

"New here, huh?" Her voice is strong.

"Yeah, first time. What's up with the name?" I point to the sign and sip my much-needed drink.

She smiles. "'Chatz' is different from your regular bar. Do you do chat rooms?"

I give her a blank stare. "Uh ... like as in a community chat room online?"

"Give me your phone." She holds out her hand. Intrigued, I reach into my purse. *Yeah, this isn't weird at all, and did I just hand over my personal phone to a complete stranger?*

She smacks her forehead. "Duh, sorry, I can be rude!" She holds out her other hand. "I'm Erin, I didn't mean to be pushy. You just looked confused reading the sign and I thought I'd come over and show you the ropes." She smiles.

I shake her hand. "Tess, and it's all right. I am curious."

"OK, so you see the scan code on the sign? You use your phone to capture it and it'll bring you to the bar's login page."

"Login page?"

"Yeah you need to create an account with a username and password, anything particular you want to be called or a nickname? Something you like to do?"

"Uh, I don't know, I just normally use my name and add a number." Judging by the look on her face, that was not good enough.

"Eh." She shrugs. "We can do better than that. Come on, give me something!"

"I like to paint and read."

"Really? That's all you can give me?" She sounds whiny. *Hey, I only came in here to relax and I'm being pressured by a complete stranger about making a screen name? Where am I?*

"Well, what's your username?" I can throw the questions just as well as she can.

She looks me square in the eye. "LuckyCharm."

It's fitting, because of her waist-length red hair and heavily lined wide green eyes.

"So you need a name that will help you stand out in a crowd like this," Erin says.

I take notice of the plush lounge setting behind me. The room is decorated in dark walls, jewel-toned velvet sofas and chairs, and women in cocktail dresses and mile-high "fuck-me" heels. The guys aren't too bad either: dress shirts, ties, full suits for some. *Where the hell am I?*

"Hello? Are you thinking of a name?" Erin pulls me from my observations, and the fact I am definitely out of my element. I'm wearing skinny jeans and a concert tee and Converse sneakers, with my hair pulled back into a low messy ponytail, for cryin' out loud!

"BEEP!" she yells. "Time's up! Here." She hands back my phone. I see the screen of other users and a name at the bottom by the text field.

"Punky_Painter?" I ask.

"Yup! You didn't want to answer me so I got bored and did it for you. And judging by your band shirt and that you like to paint ... Voila! You like?" Wow, she is a persistent thing.

"Yeah, that works, considering I'll probably never be back," I tell her. "I just stopped in to have a couple drinks and chill out, before going back to my place to work on a project and read."

"Well, in that case, the next drink is on me," Erin says.

Moments later, I have a second rum-and-coke while she sips at a margarita, She leads me to a deep red love seat and begins talking about all the people here, like she knows everyone.

"So the idea and concept is that in chat you're more secure and willing to let go. You can choose to be anyone you want to be. You call the shots on if you want to leave with someone, if not, then the person will just move on. We all have an understanding here that in the chat room we don't 'know' each other, that we think of it as role play...but we know who each other really is."

"See that girl?" Erin points to a blonde across the room, and points at my screen. "That's her, 'lawless45.'" She goes on to point out everyone in the place and their screen names.

I look at the guys in the place. Aren't they supposed to be making their rounds, trying to get numbers and drop some panties? Rather than sitting on their phones?

I watch the conversations happening on my screen. There's a lot of flirting, dates being set up, people talking about hooking up, some asking another join a "private chat," and then the two names disappear. Every now and then I notice a guy or two adjusting themselves in their seats and their pants. What is going on in those PM messages?

Erin points to another name on my screen. "See that name? 'slippery_when_wet69'?" *OK, seriously? That's just too forward. Where's the mystery?* "Yeah, I know her name is so lame, right?" I swear she can read my mind.

"Anyways, she's been with just about every guy in the room, except him." Erin discreetly nods at a guy in a dim-lit corner. She points to a name on my screen.

I roll my eyes as I read it aloud "Big_Ben? Seriously?" I know my facial expression has got to be a mix of red and contorted in the most awkward way. I try to get a better look at him, but it's so goddamned dark in this place. What makes him so immune to the girl's obvious texts?

Slippery_when_wet69: *Big_Ben come home with me baby*

Big_Ben: *Oh I don't think so*

Slippery_when_wet69: *oh common why not? *pouty face**

Big_Ben: *you know why. Now move on to your next prey.*

Huh, that's amusing to watch, especially since by the look on her face it appears she's been bitch-slapped with a meat tenderizer. And a minute later she's leaving with a guy I assume she did get her claws into. I continue to watch the "action" unfold on my phone while making small talk with Erin. Is everyone mind-fucking someone in here?

Erin breaks my train of thought. "Yeah, Big_Ben doesn't private-message with anyone, he's straightforward with the skanks of the place, and he usually leaves with one, or on a good night, two." She shrugs. "Yeah, I have seen so many of the girls here complaining about it."

"Oh" is all I could conjure up.

Erin and I continue chatting for a while; we seemed to hit it off quite easily. She goes to the same community college as me, but she's a business major and the business department is on the opposite end of campus, so that's why we have never run into one another. She tells me how she likes to come to "Chatz" for their margaritas and to just "shit around" with the guys' heads. She tells me she will only occasionally hook up with a guy, usually because of one too many margaritas, which she seems to be doing this evening seeing she's on her third now. I look at my watch and see its about midnight and decide it's time to head home. *God, I am so lame, I am not a late person, let alone one who sits at a bar all night.*

I keep my focus on this Big_Ben character, why? I'm not even sure, maybe it's my second rum and Coke doing me in. Damn, I'm such a lightweight. He seems to be chatting up a couple different users.

2Much4u2nite: *Hey Big_Ben why don't you come back to my place and I can prove my name to you?*

Big_Ben: *Well that depends, so why don't you get up and walk to the bar and I can check out what we're talking about on display?*

OK, seriously? Eew.

Just then a tall (Of course she's tall! Who isn't tall compared to my five-foot frame?) woman stalks to the bar, shaking her ass, letting it sway. I notice Erin watching too and she nudges my shoulder and rolls her eyes.

Big_Ben: *Door.*

Just as he sends that message, Miss J-Lo Booty grabs her clutch and exits. Thirty seconds later he moves from his dark corner, walks in front of Erin and myself. All that is holy and divine, he's tall, slender, dark hair and *oh my god he smells fiiiiiine... yup one too many rums...* I watch him walk to the door, and just before he pushes through, he looks right at me and I swear my heart stopped. And his face is just as glorious as his body. Strong jaw, deep but warm mocha eyes, full pouty suckable lips. His black hair screams heartbreaker. He smirks, a seriously panty-dropping smirk, and it looks devilish. *Pleasure party for one tonight! When I get home tonight greeeaaat... And then he's gone.*

"Hey, Erin, I am going to get going home. It's getting late and I would much rather curl up with my book boyfriend," I announce and stand.

She "boos" me. But grabs my phone, types something in, and hands it back. "There, now you have my number, text me anytime."

I nod and give a shy wave.

At home, text Erin to let her know I got home safe and to text me the next time she's going to Chatz. As I'm setting my phone down I notice that I never logged out of the bar's chat room before leaving.

"1 Private Message"

Curious, I click it, and it's from Big_Ben: *never seen you at Chatz before*

Chapter Two

~ Ben ~

I've been here all of ten minutes. I barely get my drink and the women are already feisty, trying to get my attention in the room. Not that I'm irritated by that fact, but after just leaving a room full of strangers staring and scrutinizing every inch of my body, I needed a few minutes to unwind. It's a little different being checked out here at a bar, because, well, let's face it, even I know I'm fucking sexy, but when you have people who are not even looking at you wanting to have sex with you, it's a little disconcerting. But my dad's new girlfriend needed a "volunteer" for her class tonight, seeing as her original setup had an emergency, and she was desperate. Man, you know how to pick 'em, Dad...

Mum passed away giving birth to my little sister Caroline when I was ten years old. I was an angry kid for a while after that, getting sent to the principal's office for fighting often and half the time, the other kid didn't even do anything wrong. What pissed me off the most was hearing the other boys talk crap about their mums for not letting them do something or have what they want. Fucking wankers were lucky to have mums. After I was expelled from two different private schools, my father was offered a job as head chief of the surgical unit at Seattle's top hospital, and we moved to the States.

Living in London, I was doing nothing but getting in trouble, and I honestly didn't give a crap on where we were going, I was fifteen when we moved. And that's when I got introduced to my best friend Dan, who was looking to start a garage band and he thought that having a dude with an accent like mine would help in the ladies' department, so that's when I learned how to play bass guitar. After that, music is the only thing that calms me down.

The hard part will be looking at my father's new girlfriend in the eye on Sunday at family dinner. I'm shaking my head in embarrassment. Yes, embarrassment. I strut to a dark area of the bar, needing to be alone for a few minutes before I give in to one these tight little bodies eyeing me. That's right, ladies, keep looking.

In a dark emerald green chair, I let my head rest on the back and close my eyes for a few seconds. I take a sip of my beer and look at my phone to see what's going on tonight. Let's see, three PM requests. Please ladies you should all know me by now decline, decline, decline... Offer number one:

TinaTaTa: *Hey Big_Ben any planes tonight? Want to tuck me in ;) ?*

Kelly84: *oh don't waste your time TinaTaTa he's coming home with me tonight, arnt ya baby?*

Wow, they are fighting over me already? Maybe I can make this work to my advantage. I wasn't looking for a threesome tonight, but I'm a trooper.

Big_Ben: *Ladies look I am here to relax tonight, but who know maybe you two might want create a group effort?*

TinaTaTa: *Sorry Big_Ben but I don't like to share.*

Aw, too bad, Tina, we could have had some fun together. Oh well, your loss, not mine...*hey where did Miss Possessive go off to? PM most likely, whatever.* The door opens and a girl I've never seen before sits at the bar. Huh. Jeans, really, here? Doesn't she know where she's at? Oh, God, that chatty LuckyCharm girl is chatting her up now.

They head to the sitting area across the room from me. Holy crap, she's short! *Compared to the redheaded chick and most of the other women here she's gotta be almost a foot shorter than the rest...kinda cute...where the fuck did that come from?*

Oh, great. Slippery_When_Wet69 is harassing me once again. How many times do I need to tell this girl that I am not interested? After what she pulled on Dan, why would I want to even share a sofa with her? Dan was one of my closest friends all through high school and even worked with me at the same magazine until he requested a location change, because he was seeing her and she was screwing around on him so much she got an STD and gave it to Dan, which thankfully he was able to catch in time. And that's only because I overheard her talking on her cell to the doctor one night outside Chatz while I was coming in for an early happy hour. "What do you mean, crabs? I can't have that. I have a boyfriend! And I barely have hair down there!" Yeah, she's that dense too. But she's been trying to get me in between the sheets for a while now. Or, hell, she'd be happy with a quickie in the alley by the trash cans.

I can't stop looking over at her, the new girl. She's so out of her element here. She's actually wearing sneakers, Chucks nonetheless. I imagine her little ass in a pair of six-inch heels, and those glasses...*Miniskirt, fuck me, my dick is twitching, what is up with me tonight?* Usually it takes a big rack and tight dress to get me all tight-panted. There's just something different about her.

Crap, I better get out of here, before I do something lame and stupid like walk over to her, ha! I can just see her face now.

2Much4u2nite: *Hey Big_Ben why don't you come back to my place and I can prove my name to you?*

Perfect timing. But I think I'm going to call it a night. I'm no longer in the mood for a clingy girl right now who whines when I leave right after sex. Besides, I have that article due tomorrow morning. I am so fortunate to have landed a job at Tones, the leading music magazine. It's even more amazing that I get to go to shows for free and interview my idols. So I don't want to fuck it up by having a late night. I reply in the open chat:

Big_Ben: *Well that depends, so why don't you get up and walk to the bar and I can check out what we're talking about on display?*

Just to make her go out the door so I can make myself look good and no leaving alone. Hey, I do have a reputation to uphold. If I can just get her to leave, then I'll follow out the door and explain to the girl how I just remembered I have some place to be and make my escape on my bike. Yeah, that'll do.

I make it a point to walk past this new creature, just to let her have a full look at the package, to moisten those panties. I strut right in front of her, and oh yeah, she noticed. I stop at the door, and for some reason I feel the need to look back, and when I do I see her staring at me. Her face just seriously turned red. Yeah, watch this, inducing panty-dropping smile in 3...2...1...*Oh yeah. And I am out.*

I pop in my headphones and click on one of my favorite playlists, throw on my helmet, and throttle off.

At my place, I suddenly feel lonely. I don't feel lonely that often, but thinking about my mum tonight kind of did me in. It's too late to call my baby sister to see how her day went. After mum passed away, we were always together. I like watching over her. I fish out my cell and log back into Chatz and create a private message. I'm breaking my one rule when it comes to girls, but she's not like any other girl I have seen in a long long time.

Chapter Three

Tess

Oh my God. Who is banging around at this hour of the morning? What time is it? And why do I feel like I want to die? I roll over in my bed to look at the clock on my nightstand. 11:53. “CRAP!” I am so going to be late to work. I cannot afford to be late again or Susan, my boss, will fire me for real this time. Yeah, she has been trying to fire me for the last six months, but she loves me too much for that. But I don’t want to keep letting her down either...

I take the world’s fastest shower, dress with wet hair, grab my bag and keys, and I am out. Time: ten minutes, thirteen seconds! OWNED!

I stumble on one of the stone steps leading up to the coffee shop door. Yup, epic frailer and walking disaster, all rolled up into one short package. It doesn’t go unnoticed, but most of the customers know that I am a walking calamity. They just shake their heads. I look behind the counter at Dave, my co-worker.

"So how's my short stuntman doing this afternoon? I say afternoon, because you are twenty minutes late when you were supposed to be here at noon." Dave states matter-of-factly, while purses his highly glossed lips, seriously dude, gloss? Dave can be a bit personal and pushy sometimes, always wanting to get together to hang out with me after work or the status update on my love life YEAH, WHAT LOVE LIFE? But he makes work interesting by offering up random challenges. Whoever loses has to do the most complex order brought our way. You know the order I am talking about: the "I'll need two café lattes, one large with an extra shot, caramel, non-fat, no whip, the second is a medium decaf soy, no room for foam and cinnamon." My unspoken retort: You'll get what I give you and I'll say I got it right.

My shift goes by pretty quickly, probably because I keep refilling my triple shot macchiato more than a few times. I feel like I need a padded room, because I am about to start bouncing off the freaking walls!

"So what are your plans for the rest of your evening, baby doll?" Dave asks as we are about to lock the doors. He asks me this after every shift we work together, and honestly is getting tiresome, but I like him so I deal. Dave and I have been working together for about two years now and have gotten somewhat close. We tend to talk a lot about his love life and his male flavor of the week. Sometimes he acts so stereotypically gay that you would have to think he MUST be acting, but what straight man in his right mind would pretend to be gay? Let alone for the last two years I have known him?

I wrap my jacket close around me, because it's so freakin' cold out. "I'm just going to head home, crank my stereo and paint all night, that's just what I do every Saturday night, unless there's a good rock show going on."

"Oh yeah? That's cool, I'm more of a country kind of guy myself," Dave admits. Huh, did not know that, and wouldn't have guessed by looking at him. Dave is about five-eleven, very slender, with moppy blond hair.

"Look, I am heading to this club a few blocks away tonight. YOU should meet me there," he suggests.

I scrunch up my face. "Not much of a club girl. I'm a 'go home, read, paint and crank the tunes' kind of girl." I hate the idea of clubs: small dance floor crowded by sweaty horny people, rubbing up on each other. I don't think so.

"All right. Maybe another time, something more 'Tess.'" Dave sounds hopeful. "How about we just hang out at your place instead? I'll bring something you can refuse." His tone is off by this point and frankly I just want to get home.

He waves a weak goodbye and walks off. I hop to it and walk fast to my car, with my keys in between my fingers in case anyone decides to maul me. I am ready to go all Catwoman on their asses...*yeah right I'd probably scream like a girl and drop.* As I unlock my car door and open it, I drop my keys, and I feel the buzz of my cell phone in my back pocket, I look around, because I have seen enough movies to know that when a girl drops her keys in a parking lot, she gets attacked as soon as she bends to pick them up. So I look around first. *That's right, Tess, stay one step ahead.* I get, in close my door and fish out my phone. It's a text from Erin.

Erin: *"Hey! What are you doing tonight? Do you wanna hang?"*

I reply: *"I'm not in the mood to go out night, I just got off work, but you are more than welcome to come by my place, I'll order a pizza."*

Erin: "*Sounds awesome! Send me your address.*"

After I text my address, I click to get off of my messages and there it is, the message I forgot all about from last night. Damn rum. "Big_Ben: '*I've never seen you at Chatz before,*'" I read out loud. What am I supposed to do? Do I message him back, even though it's been nearly twenty-four hours? Maybe Erin can help me figure out this mystery.

As I get back to my place with the pizza, Erin is pulling in behind me. I wave her over and we walk up to my studio. When I open the door, Erin pretty much gasps, "You live here?"

"Um yeah..." I say. "I know it's a little small, but it's all I can afford on a barista's pay, but I get all the coffee I can dream of, so it balances out."

Erin smiles as she takes her pea coat off and walks to my teeny-weeny kitchen, and faces out to the rest of the small space. "Are all these paintings and photographs yours?" she asks.

"Yep."

"Wow, you really don't go out often, do you?" she says, shaking her head, but with a smile so I don't take any offense. I like Erin, she's honest and forward, the perfect kind of friend. The kind that won't bullshit you, then turn around and talk behind your back.

"Oh!" I yell. "That reminds me." I show Big_Ben's private message to Erin.

"This is crazy! Seriously, he just doesn't do that!

What did you say?" She's practically screaming at me.

I shrug. "Nothing yet. I don't know what to do or say, if anything."

Erin starts bouncing from one foot to another. "Oh, you HAVE to say something! Here send him a message right now! Find out what he wants!"

She practically throws the phone at me. "But what do I say?"

"I don't know, act casual and leave some mystery. Men love mystery." If that's the case, why do they always go for the girls who show more flesh in a public venue than on a private beach? And are so forward with their come-ons? Yeah, they gotta love a mystery woman.

I roll my eyes, and as I punch at the little buttons I read aloud. "No, you haven't." Send.

"There ya go, girl, put the ball in his court." She winks. "Now we wait."

I open up the pizza box and pull out a couple of plates. "Well, while we do, let's grab some food and pop in a movie."

Erin scans my collection of mostly romance comedies, pulls one out, and pops it in. I come around with the food and drink, and we stretch out on the floor with one of my favorites: *"The Perfect Man."*

Erin chats randomly about the guys she's dated, and I chat about my lack thereof. She's been dating since she was fourteen. Her parents didn't really set any rules for her; they apparently thought their little girl was an angel. "Can you believe that they thought I was still a virgin on graduation day? If only they knew how many guys I had blown." She let out a robust laugh and winks at me. *Oh my.*

She finally controls her laughter. "So how many guys have you slept with?"

I almost spit out my soda. Man, she doesn't hold back, does she? "Uh...none."

Her mouth gapes open at my response. "Are you serious right now? Never? Ever?"

I just shake my head. I am not used to sex talk. She is still shocked, but continues her game of twenty-one questions. "Fooled around with?"

"None." I am not ashamed to be a virgin, but the way it's so glorified these days, society outcasts you if you have a hymen after the age of fifteen.

"So you mean to tell me you have never screwed or blew a guy?" she asks, kind of crudely, but I don't mind. I like this about Erin.

I straighten my posture and look her dead in the eye. "Never even touched a guy's thing either." And with that her and I both burst out into laughter.

She wipes a tear away from her eye. "God, I hope you at least have a good vibrator!"

I can feel my face go red. "No, I don't have one, never have. I honestly don't masturbate much. I don't know, never felt that strong of an urge to." The look on Erin's face is priceless.

"Oh man, I wish I had your restraint! If I don't get fucked in a day I at least reach for my goodie drawer in my nightstand." She's dead serious. I love her already for being so open about her sexuality.

I look her right in the eye. "Nympho." And she whips the pillow from behind her right at me, almost causing me to spill my wine.

"Hey! What did the wine ever do to you? Don't go hurtin' my baby!" You mess with my wine, caffeine, paint, music, or my camera you better prepare to feel my wrath.

We finally settle back down and get back into the movie.

Just as Heather Locklear's character is chatting to Hilary Duff's soon-to-be boyfriend on the computer, when my phone chimes. Yeah, kind of ironic timing. We look at each other and dive for the phone at the same time, but I beat her to it. HA! I look at the screen and it says *"1 private message"* I click it and read "Big_Ben: *So why haven't I seen you there before?"*

Erin is right over my shoulder. "Well, say something!"

Punky_Painter: *Well that's, because it was my first time there*

Big_Ben: *Well now why is that?*

Punky_Painter: *Because I'm not typically a social drinker.*

Erin is practically coming out of her skin, she's so giddy with excitement. I have never felt my heart beat so fast. Well, in a good way, anyways.

Big_Ben: *Well maybe you should stop by a little more*

OK, that got me a little leery. I mean, I don't want to openly flirt with someone in a chat room full of scantily clad bimbos. *Well, they say honesty is the best policy so...*

Punky_Painter: *Nothing wrong with the place, but I saw your chats with some of the girls there and I am not into a one night stand or to publically embarrass myself.*

Yeah, take that. Really, I'm not being unreasonable or hard to get.

Big_Ben: *Well then aren't you feisty, why don't you come on down to Chatz and tell me that yourself, if you're so sure.*

Punky_Painter: *Well because for one, I have no intention of having sex tonight and I have company and we are quite comfortable.*

Erin hops to her knees and thrusts her hips and moans. Oh my God. Can she be any funnier?

Big_Ben: *Well they can't be very good company if you're not having sex tonight and your sitting on your phone talking with me.*

Punky_Painter: *And why is that? I heard you don't do private chats?*

I swear if Erin could dislocate her jaw it would be on my floor.

Big_Ben: *I don't.*

Punky_Painter: *So what do you call this?*

Big_Ben: *Meet me at the bar.*

Punky_Painter: *I told you no I have company.*

And with that I turned off my phone. I looked over at Erin; she is wide-eyed and holding her chest. "Why aren't we going?" she practically screams at me.

"I told him I had company, and I don't know about you but I am enjoying my company." I wink at her.

She lets out a big sigh. "Yeah I am, don't get me wrong or anything. But you have to admit that was kind of exciting."

I look away and I can feel my cheeks flush a little. "Yeah, it was."

Chapter Four

~ Ben ~

Wow, she said no? No one has ever turned me down. But then again, she wasn't all over me at the bar the other night. She wasn't dressed like the other women there, and she wasn't there for a hookup, which is why most people go to Chatz to begin with. Now I have to know why she was there. Question is, how I am going to get her to meet me there or anywhere now that someone has apparently given her all the details on my reputation. Crap. And what's even crappier is that I have my family dinner tomorrow.

Before leaving for my traditional Sunday night family dinner, I decide to call Dan and check in with him. "Hey man! What's new?" I ask my best friend.

"Oh, same ol', same ol'. You know the routine: Sleep, eat, work...well in your case: sleep, eat, work, and screw." He always likes to rag on me about my sexual endeavors. "So, what type of girl did you nail last night?"

"None." I confess.

Silence fills the dead air on the phone line. "What do you mean none? Are you sick? Is everyone OK? It takes devastation to for you to keep it in your pants!"

Ugh, I have to talk about with someone. "There's this woman...She came into the bar last night and well she's not what I typically go for."

"And...?" He urges me on.

"And, I may have sent her a private message."

"DUDE! This is major! You never do that! Awww someone's getting married!" He teases.

Tensing up at the word, "No. I don't think so. Maybe I just had one too many that night." I try to reason.

"When did you meet this girl?"

"Friday night after Gwen's class."

I can practically hear the gears in his head spinning. "What made her so different? And why didn't you make a move? I mean no one has said no to you before." Yeah, don't I know it?

"Well she's not like any of the other women I have been with. You know my type. This girl, she's short, wears glasses, came in wearing jeans and a t-shirt and get this, Chucks." I spill.

He lets out a hearty laugh on the other end "Yeah, definitely not the type you go after." Dan goes quiet again, this can't be good. "So, you're telling me that you haven't banged a girl for two, count them TWO days? What about today?"

Agitated now that my best friend doesn't think I have any self-control. "NO! None in three fucking days, OK?" I know I shouldn't snap at Dan, considering he's the only person who knows the real me and how I operate. Maybe it's the lack of sex...

"All right! Got it man, I'll drop it. It's just unlike you that's all, kind of proud honestly. I mean since the whole Nicole thing." He's sincere.

"Yeah. Thanks." I don't want to even continue on with that subject, so I turn it around. "When are you going to find the 'right girl' as you like to put it?"

"I'll know when I see her." Ugh, someone needs to have their ovaries removed.

Dan starts laughing at my obvious tone of disgust. "One day you'll try it again."

"Whatever. Hey I gotta get to my Dad's place, when are you coming back into town?" I am eager to have a few beers and a jam session.

"In a few weeks actually."

"Awesome. Sounds good dude." And we sound off.

Me in a serious relationship? He is freaking mad.

I pull into my father's driveway on my bike, and look up at the semi-mansion on the cushy cul-de-sac. I liked it here. Dan lived just down the strip, so getting together every day to work on our band skills was pretty awesome. It was a safe community, a typical neighborhood.

Well I may as well face Dad's girlfriend, after her Friday class.

I walk in and Caroline rushes me and gives me a tight hug. She's fifteen now, growing up, but she's still my baby sister. She's about half a foot shorter than I am now, *man when did she sprout up?* She is definitely getting older. Instead of braided pigtails she now has a chin length bob with bangs. With her hair as black as mine and rouge lipstick, she is reminding me of a nineteen-twenties flapper. "Benji! Thank God you're finally here! I was dying listening to her talk nonstop about her class and her adventures in the sixties."

"Well, I am here now and it's time for me to feel embarrassed too..." Caroline hasn't exactly had the picture perfect childhood, after we moved to the states she in a way shut off. She was young when we made the move and I know it was a big change for her. I know it wasn't just Dad's job offer here that prompted our sudden move, but because of my troubles at the other schools and law. But recently she's been more distant, which is odd considering we were so close years ago. I'll have to pull her aside later to find out what's up.

We walk through the foyer to the kitchen to find our father with his arms wrapped around Gwen's waist from behind as they look out the kitchen window.

"Hey Dad," I announce when we walk into the large chef's dream kitchen. They turn in unison. It isn't odd to see Dad with a woman; he's had his fair share since mum passed away. He didn't jump right into dating, though. It took him about five years before he could even look at a woman, but once some of the wounds had healed he tried to find his perfect match again, with a few flings in between. He explained that no one would ever compare to our mum, that she was beyond beautiful, and she was classy and full of life.

"Hello Ben," Gwen greets me with a wink. Oh God, here we go, and as long as these two are together I am never going to live this down.

I take in a deep breath. "Hey Gwen, I hope your students were able to accomplish what you wanted."

"Well, you know I need you to come back to the class tomorrow so my students can finish their drawings," she said with a huge grin. Yeah, how could I forget about going back to a classroom with twenty or so students staring at my naked body as I sit up on display for them?

"Yeah, I know, I won't forget and I will be there." I give her a reassuring nod.

After dinner we all move into the living room. Dad talks about his recent achievements at the hospital. A big award was presented to his surgical unit, along with a rather large donation. But what catches my attention is how attentive he is with Gwen. I can't remember the last time I saw him so attracted to a woman he was seeing. It's just sort of odd, because they are polar opposites. Dad is a successful doctor and she is a community college art professor. Well, I always hear "opposites attract," so why not in this case? As long as she isn't a gold digger, like the last girlfriend.

Caroline excitedly tells us all about this summer fashion program she applied to in New York City. Apparently she would get to help out a few up-and-coming designers by fetching materials, making calls, and sorting mail. This is apparently huge to Caroline. She has always been a fashion freak; since she was three she was picking out her own clothes and trying new things. By eight, she was designing clothes and began learning how to sew. Now, at fifteen, her whole closet is full of her creations, and I'll even admit they aren't half bad (and I'm so happy they're nothing like the girls at the bars wear!)

"So Benjamin how's the magazine doing?" Dad asks. He has always supported my interest in music. Hell, he told me all about the old-school punk shows he would sneak into as a teen in London. He even bought me my first bass. But expected me to do that kind of thing in my free time and ultimately I think the bass was a bribe to get me to even go to college. Eventually Dad grudgingly accepting my choice to study writing, Dad wanted me to follow in his footsteps. To be a real career man, a doctor like him. This was always a sore subject that usually ended with us ignoring my career of choice or me storming out in a rage.

"Really good, I have a few shows coming up to cover and I'll be interviewing the bands." I love my job and I know it shows on my face. I am proud of what a success the magazine has become. And even when I'm not set up for work I still go to as many rock shows as I can.

"You know Ben, when are you going to come to realize that writing about a band for a column isn't going to last you your whole life. Eventually your boss will want to hire someone younger, more up with the changing music? That they will let you go without a second thought? Then what? What will you do for the rest of your life to fall back on?" My Dad rambles the same speech at least every other month.

I suck in a deep breath preparing to recite my typical lines on the subject. "Dad, I don't know how long this will last or where it will take me. That's the adventure in it. I don't want to be hog tied down in a position that not only brings amazing outcomes for your patients, but so much heartache and devastation. I can't do that to good people. To have that much trust set in your hands, with the risk of messing up and killing someone, I... I just couldn't handle that."

He looks like he's about to set his standing argument when I finish what I want to say, "I may not write for *Tones* forever and that's fine. But I will always write and I hope it's about music, but if not that's fine, because I'll still be doing what I love."

I look from my father who is starting to stand to leave, just as he always does, when my eyes meet Caroline's. She looks blank and her eyes teary. "Caroline? Are you alright?" I ask my sister.

She blinks, rubs her wrists and nods at me before replying, "Yeah, I'm fine, just a lot of stuff on my mind. School stuff you know." Her voice is soft and dull. Non-Caroline. She darts her eyes to our father, who is looking at her. "Dad doesn't want me to go to New York this summer." She states.

That's all it took for dad to blow up "You know why that is Caroline! Do you know how many people actually get jobs in the fashion field? Where they can make an honest living? Hmm? Not many, I can tell you that. Now if you were to focus more on your science studies, well now that's where you could excel."

"I don't want to be a doctor Dad." She responds to our father with a lifeless tone. It breaks my heart, because I know exactly what she's going through with him. Hell that's why I rebelled so much back in London. When mum passed he got real strict.

Not being able to stand seeing her take his crap anymore tonight I stand, "Let's go sit out back for a few, it's nice out." I suggest. She stands and we make our way out the patio doors in the kitchen to the large deck out back.

She nods and wipes a single tear from her face with the back of her wrist, her gray sweater absorbing the moisture.

Once outside I speak, "I know it's tough with Dad, and you know I know how bad it gets. But just remember before you know it, it'll be summer and you'll be in New York putting your foot in the door of your dream. You can do this Caroline, I believe in you. This will be the best thing for you."

I see a spark of hope in her eyes, "And before you know it, you'll be living in New York going to fashion school. Just listen to your heart and a little less of Dad. Hell I had to."

Chapter Five

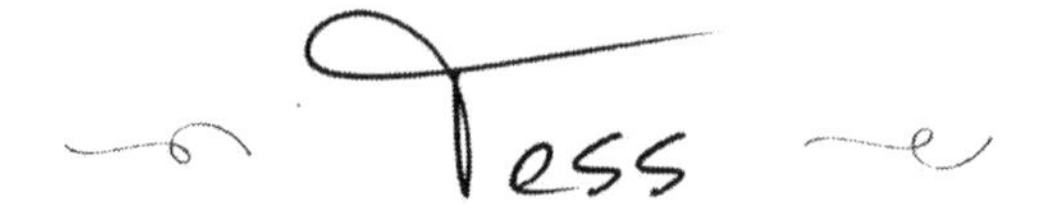

I got to sleep in this Monday morning for once, because I didn't have a shift at the coffee shop. It's just as well. I'm too distracted. I can't stop seeing the image of Big_Ben's sexy smile as he left Chatz with that other girl. I had some tea. I cranked up my music and busted out my paints. I sang, I danced around, and I got paint all over. How exactly one get paint in their armpit?

Before I know it, it's time to get to class. Seeing as we are continuing with the beefcake of a man from last week, and I am determined to not be late today! I want a better spot and a better view. I got dressed in my black and red striped skinny jeans and my cute black peplum top with a thin red belt and my over the knee boots. Yeah, I may be trying a lot for this class, but why not? I threw on a little mascara and lip gloss.

In the parking lot, I see a few of my female classmates also got a little dressed up, probably trying to catch the attention of the dark-haired hunk. Well, at least I'm not the only one. But what was I thinking, that I could even compare to the girls in my class?

Inside, I see a spot in the front. Score! I don't see the model yet, but I pass Ms. Sawyer coming towards the classroom. "Ah, Tess, I am glad to see you on time!"

To calm myself down I decided to put one ear bud in and turn on my iPod. Music is the only calming thing except for wine and rum, and I am pretty sure that's frowned upon on school property.

Ms. S instructs us to begin.

I look up.

I let out a big gasp, and then he looks right at me...

It's him! Holy crap, it's Big_Ben! What the hell?! Oh my effing God! And he's naked! *Well, duh dummy! That's why you're here! To DRAW him!*

He looks as shocked as I am. But I am not looking away. My eyes begin to travel and he notices when I stop below his waist. He is sitting partially upright, leaning his upper body up against what looks like an overstuffed beanbag chair, probably from Ms. S's own house.

The lower part of his body is bent at the waist and one leg is arched, with his knee towards the ceiling, where the other is bent, but lying on the table. And there *he* is. Right. In. The. Open. I can't move, I can't look away, but then I hear a throat clearing and I look up at his face, and he winks at me. Holy crap, he just winked at me! I know my face is red, I can feel it. I can also feel the heat from my cheeks spread down my body. I quickly look down at my sketchbook, pick up one of my pencils, and attempt to look anywhere but *there*. So I start with his head, and when I look up at him he is still looking at me! How am I going to do this for an hour?

So I just start. I don't make eye contact but I can feel his eyes on me the entire time. His body is slender but sculpted, and the tattoos that I had noticed during last week's class carry over to his pecs. He also has art on the outer parts of his forearms. His abs are defined, but not bulging, with a happy little trail leading down to his, well...impressive size. And I swear as I am looking at him there attempting to focus and do him justice, I think I see him twitch... all sixty minutes of the class.

When Ms. S tells us that our time is up, I look down at my drawing and I am quite pleased with it. I got the shading and proportions right on. The only thing I didn't finish was his face; I just couldn't bring myself to look up at his face, knowing he was looking at me the entire time. I close my sketchbook and pack up my pencils as fast as I can, while this amazingly gorgeous man hops down from the table. Most of the class has already left, minus a few of the other girls, who are watching him grab a sheet to wrap around his waist.

"Benjamin, will you wait a moment before taking off?" Ms. S asks him. He nods and walks over to the corner.

As I am about to leave, Ms. S asks the same of me. Why oh why can't I just escape?

"Tess, will you show me your sketch, please?" I oblige. She studies it for a moment and says, "Benjamin, you can go on into the back room and get dressed, but don't leave just yet, please."

She takes my book and looks it over. "I knew you had it in you, Tess! This is outstanding! Although I see you haven't finished the face. I noticed you avoiding it earlier, so that's why I have asked you to stay behind."

Crap. Where is she going with this?

He walks out from the back room in a pair of jeans, a light gray fitted V-neck tee, and black boots, carrying the same black leather jacket he was wearing at Chatz on Friday night. He's heading for the door. But Ms. S steps in front of him. "Ben, I would like to have you stay for a few extra minutes so one of my students can finish her sketch. All she needs is to observe your face." As she stops talking she looks over at me across the room.

His eyes shoot to mine and I die. No really, my heart just stopped. OK, not really, but it certainly feels like it did. "Ben, this is Tess, one of my most talented students, so this is why I would like her to finish her piece," Ms. S explains, handing him my sketchbook. Crap.

"Of course, Gwen, that's fine." Oh God he's British! Can my panties drop any faster? He has a wicked grin as he looks down at my drawing of him, studies it for a second, and walking towards me. Holy crap, he's stalking towards me...I think I need fresh panties. Oh. My. God.

“Hi, I’m Ben.” He extends his right hand, waiting for me to return the gesture. I fumble with my bag and drop it. As I bend to pick it up, he reaches it first, stands, and hands it back to me. I set it in the chair next to me and turn back to him.

“I believe this is yours.” He’s handing my book back to me.

I blush. “Thanks. Um, I’m...” I take my sketchbook.

“Punky_Painter?” he asks me with a wink.

And I come back with, “Big_Ben? Seriously?” I look down to his pants and shrug a little, not that I have seen many—OK, none till now, except in a movie or two. But I’d best be keeping him on his toes.

He smirks and says, “Yeah, well...” I have no idea what to say to that.

He sits in front of where I am sitting about a foot away. Yeah, kind of close. Ugh, he smells so good... “I guess I’ll just sit pretty ‘til you finish your drawing. And I want to thank you for doing me justice in my boys’ department,” he adds, sounding cocky.

I just sit and blush. And draw. What do you say to a complete sex god sitting in front of you and you have all the rights in the world to stare at him and do what you love best—create? Hmm...wonder if he’d mind if I put my headphones in. Can’t hurt to ask...

“Do you mind if I listen to some music?” I ask shyly.

"No, of course not. How long do you think you need to stare at my face? No rush or anything, I was just curious." Wow, he's being kind? I stand and pull my iPod out of my back pocket. I can feel his eyes scan over my body and I feel my knees start to shake, so I quickly sit my butt back down. I unravel my headphone cords and just as I am about to pop the buds in my ears, he speaks up.

"Oh you're not going to let me listen?" He asks with a little bit of a pouty face. It melts my heart. I don't know how serious he's being right now, but either way I like it a little better than purposely trying to embarrass me.

I look right into his eyes. "Well, I don't know what kind of music you like and I don't want to sicken you and make your face scrunch up while I am trying to draw it."

"Try me," he challenges. Oh really, I would like to. Maybe run my tongue from the tip if your chin and taste that freshly grown stubble down your neck, then make my way all the way down to that happy little trail of yours...*Snap out of it, girl!* Fine, if he wants to play this game I will play too. Hmm...what playlist to put on...let's see how he likes a little bit of Britney, bitch! I click onto the play list and hit play. The song "Womanizer" comes up first and I think he's about to piss himself by the look on his face! Oh, this is too funny! He chuckles and shakes his head and just when I think he's about to protest he surprises me.

"You're a womanizer oh, womanizer oh, womanizer baby..." And he keeps humming with the tune! Holy shit! He knows Britney songs! Oh, I did not expect that and he can tell I am shocked off my rocker.

"I wouldn't have taken you as a Britney fan," I tell him, without looking up from my work.

"I wouldn't have guessed you were one either," he shoots back, "although I can never tell when it comes to girls. But then again everything about you so far surprises me." Huh. I didn't expect that answer. I guess my mystery level is satisfactory. Erin would be proud. He's coming off as honest, not like the bad boy his appearance gives off. But I'm not going to let that take the lead. I don't trust easily and with good reason. If he wants in he's going to have to beg and prove himself worthy...that is, if he even wants to...

"So why the message on Friday night? Didn't you leave with someone? That couldn't have made her too happy to see you messaging someone else, because I know if it were me..." *Shut up Tess! Shut Up! You're rambling again! Why did you have so much tea before class? You know what caffeine does to you and your mouth!*

He interrupts me by simply smiling. I am now mush. Oh wow. Yup, I am a total girl right now. "So who told you I don't do private messages?"

"Well, a newfound friend from Chatz. She kind of had to explain the whole setup to me," I confess.

He lets out a breath, and I put my pencil back to the paper. "Well, your friend is right, I don't do private messages. Ever. I just don't see the point. If I just want to fuck and they just want to fuck, why be so private about it? I mean, why do we have to kid ourselves into thinking it's something special and private? If I leave with a girl, then people already know that we are about to go hook up, so why hide it even in the beginning?"

"Oh," is all I can muster up. He just sits quietly. I'm not so much in the mood for Britney anymore, so I pick up my iPod and hand it to him. That's as private as you can get with me. Why shouldn't I be a little more giving? He just told me that he doesn't do private anything, and yet he did with me.

He looks me in the eyes and back down at the device in my hand. "You sure?" He looks a little leery.

"Go ahead, whatever you want to listen to." This is my own little challenge to see what he's into. He takes it and begins scrolling through my large collection. Looking impressed he hits a button, and "Girls and Boys" from Good Charlotte begins to fill the air. I snort. Of course he would pick a song that talks about how guys like girls who fake and made of plastic, but who cares as long as they are gorgeous and are willing to put out.

"What?" He laughs and shrugs.

I shake my head and mumble, "I bet you do." He squints his eyes and looks completely serious for a moment but before he can open his mouth I continue "I saw the girls at the bar, total plastic bimbos, especially the ones you seemed to be, for lack of better words, really chatty with." Oh, I got him on that one.

His jaw snaps open "Oh I see. You think you know me by one measly song choice and the fact that I was talking to a few women in a chat room? How fair is that?"

Great, now I feel like crap. He goes on, "... and if you listen to the song you'd hear how girls will take whatever they can get from a guy and don't give a shit about them. Did you ever stop to think that maybe those girls were using me?" Whoa! That came out of nowhere! "I'm sorry, I didn't mean to jump on you like that. I don't know why I did."

"I'm sorry I assumed," I say, finish the drawing, and pack up. He's rubbing his face with his hands like he's exasperated. "Thank you for staying long enough to let me finish, and again sorry I said anything."

"Look, I don't talk about myself much, and people assume way too much about me. They have my whole life, but it wasn't right of me to jump down your throat." He drops his head and shakes it for a moment. I start to walk for the door, and he's quickly at my back.

"Can I help you?" I ask him, without turning around. He lightly touches my elbow and chills shoot through me. My body is hit with a wild fire. I slowly turn to face him. *Yep, mush.* He's so close I can feel his breath on my face. He puts his hands on the door jamb next to both sides of my face and leans into me, but avoids touching me.

With his eyes closed, he says, "I don't know. Can you?"

Chapter Six

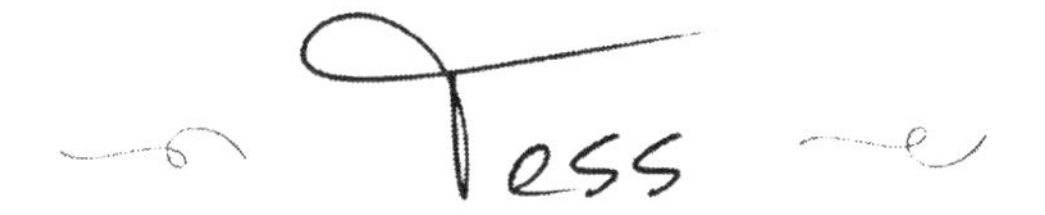

It takes all the strength I have not to wrap myself around him. He's so close I can feel him, smell him, and almost taste him. He finally unpins me from the wall, dropping his hands to his sides, and I practically run out the door. Surprisingly, my legs don't give out. Once I am down the hall a little way I round the corner and lean against the cool brick. Breathless.

Holy shit! What was that? One minute he's kind and intriguing, then he's cocky and snapping at me, and then he was all over me. If I had stayed there one minute longer, would he have kissed me? I guess I'll never know now. I let out the largest sigh of my life once I reach my car. I climb in and pull out my phone to text Erin: *You busy?*

Almost immediately she answers: "*Nope, free as a bird, what ya got in mind?*" God as little time as I have known this girl, I feel like she's my lifesaver.

I text back: "*My place, bring wine...or something stronger!*"

She replies with a thumbs-up emoticon.

Back at my studio, I plop down on the red couch and put my head in my hands. My phone vibrates, alerting me to a message: 1 Private Message. No way can it be him! There's no way after what had happened. I click it to open the message:

Big_Ben: *I am once again sorry for the way I acted; I hope you can forgive me.*

I'm awestruck. This is one of the most confusing guys I have ever met. Not that I have met many, but damn, he's messing with my head. Why does it matter? I'll probably never be forced to see him again. I don't know if that pleases me or depresses me.

Punky_Painter: *You don't have to apologize. It seems irrelevant, considering we won't have to see each other again.*

Big_Ben: *Don't be so sure of that.*

And that's how I am going to leave it, because frankly he kind of scares the crap out of me with those whiplash mood swings. And thank God for Erin knocking on my door to break this feeling in the pit of my stomach. I rush to the door and before I even open it, I am yelling, "You are never going to believe who was the model in my class..." and I open the door to find HIM standing there.

Silence quickly overcomes me.

"So who was this model from your class?" He asks with his head tipped down, looking at me through dark hooded eyelashes.

Still in a mind slump, all I can think of is, "Um...how did you get my address?"

He looks to his left down the hall and Erin comes into view. *What the hell?* She steps into my apartment and shrugs in an apologetic way, not too convincingly, I might add.

Erin the traitor finally speaks after a moment. "Look, he ran into me when I was leaving campus and stopped me. He knew me from Chatz and he looked a little rough so when he asked me if he could ask a question, I couldn't say no," she explains. *Oh, yes you very damn well could!*

"So you showed him where I lived? What if he's a serial killer or a rapist?" I gasp. I am freaking out at this point. I am a really private person and this oversteps all the security issues I have with guys since the '*incident*'. I look from him to her and I try to figure out what the hell I am going to do. Flee. I practically run to my bathroom and close the door.

"Tess!" Erin yells from the other side of the door. "What are you doing?" I can imagine her throwing her arms up in the air and pacing the floor, but what I can't imagine is *him* standing in my home, looking at my personal stuff...god my paintings.

"Is he still out there?" I ask, while pinching the bridge of my nose.

I hear a masculine groan and, “Yeah I am.”

“Why?”

A knock on the door makes me fall back slightly. Wow I didn’t even notice I was standing so close to the door...

“Can we talk?”

“Go ahead.” I throw my hands up over my head, but he obviously can’t see that.

He turns the knob. *DAMN IT! I forgot to lock the door behind me!* I lunge at the door, but he’s already stepping in before I reach it. Crap.

“Look, I felt really bad the way we left things. Hell, I don’t even know why I am really here. This is really unlike me, but I couldn’t get through the night before I could at least try and explain myself...or understand this myself...” He motions the space between us but mumbles the last part under his breath.

I untangle my arms from around my chest and step back toward the shower, giving him room to enter. Are we seriously having a conversation in my bathroom? “Go ahead.” I gesture with my hand.

He looks like he’s about to speak when I throw my hands to my mouth. “Erin!” He whips his head back to the door as I come to realize my new best friend is in my living room probably feeling used and abandoned, maybe imagining some dirty bathroom scene.

I streak past Ben and rush out to the small living space, but instead I run right into Erin. Umph! We tumble to the floor and start laughing.

"Were you listening through the door?" I ask her, attempting to look serious.

She bats her eyes and pouts, "But whatever do you mean?" in her best Southern belle voice, while fanning herself with her hand.

"Yeah, yeah, save it, traitor," I accuse her, while standing up and offering her my hand to help her up.

She straightens her shirt and grabs her bag off my counter. "Well, now that you have company, I guess I'll be going." She actually winks at me.

"What do you mean, you're leaving?" I yank her to the side and get really up close and personal with her ear. "What am I supposed to do? I don't know why he's here or what he has planned and you're seriously going to leave me here ALONE?" I yank on her arm a little.

I'll admit I am excited and frankly a little giddy about being alone with him, but I am still having a hard time believing it, and believing what I might do when it happens. But, then again, what did almost happen that night was in a very crowded space...so what's the difference? Guess I am about to find out.

It's her turn to get a little too close, and all she has to say is, "bow-chicka-wow-wow." While gyrating her hips ever so slightly. My face goes white... or should I say *whiter*.

"We can talk later if you'd prefer. I didn't mean to ruin any plans you had for the evening. I wasn't thinking." Ben steps forward and puts his hands in his jeans pockets, accentuating his toned arms. But it's the look on his face that I can't get over. His features are hard but soft at the same time. He looks derailed and unsure of himself. I find this odd, considering he has been nothing but upfront and pushy. I take notice of his caramel mocha eyes. They are the most amazing and delicious set of eyes I have seen...*Yeah, I am a coffee addict, aren't I? Then again I think I just found my new addiction...*

Erin steps to the door. "No, you two obviously have some tension that needs to be resolved. I don't know what it is and I am sure that's why *I* was *invited* over tonight...to find out." She elevates her voice when she says I and invited to make her point...what is her point? She volunteers to leave even when Ben offered to take a rain check. I don't know if I want to hug her or slap her. I am about to protest, but she's out the door. I am alone with him. Double crap.

Chapter Seven

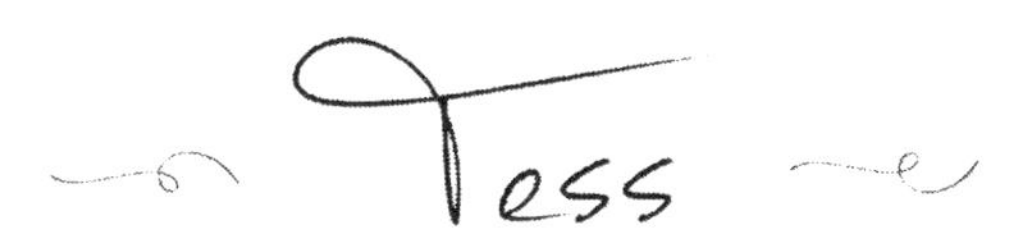

I slowly turn to see him leaning against my small counter. His tall lean body makes my studio apartment look even more minuscule. He's still wearing his fitted light gray t-shirt and the way he's standing, I can see every ripple of his tight chest and his lean abs. I unconsciously lick my lips. He straightens up and walks towards me. I can feel my breath quicken and my face flush and the next thing I know his arms are around me and I am being lowered onto my couch...what the...

"Hey, you OK? You got really pale and you started to slump against the door like you were passing out."

Yeah, I can die now from embarrassment. "Oh, I am fine. I'm probably just hungry and it's really hot it here. Are you hot?" I start to ramble. Not good.

"No, I am cool. Want me to grab you something from the kitchen?" He asks me while he's already walking away. "A banana would probably be good for you."

Food does sound really good right about now, so I nod. He's back to my side right away, handing me the banana. I begin peeling it back, and catch him staring at me as I begin to take a bite.

"What?" I ask with a mouthful.

He looks back at me with a small smile. "Oh nothing." And then I put it together... *Yeah. ha ha, funny. I'm eating a banana.* I roll my eyes and finish.

"What? Have something against bananas?" I nudge his shoulder with my own. He lets out a light laugh and shakes his head.

"So what did you need to talk to me about that made you hound my friend and bust out your inner stalker to find my apartment?" I ask.

His head falls to the back of my sofa and looks at me. "Well, like I said I wanted to apologize for my behavior back at the school. I had no reason to snap at you the way I did and then hold you against your will." Oh, believe me, it wasn't against my will. In fact it took all of my willpower not to pounce on him right then and there!

"Well, I guess I should apologize for not properly introducing myself...Tess." I hold out my hand this time and he takes it. "Ben. Ben Mitchell. It's nice to meet you, Tess."

He leaves his hand in mine and I don't mind in the slightest. It's giving me the chills yet my body is on fire. He's rubbing his thumb over the back of my hand and the fire ignites low in my belly, causing my muscles to clench in a way I didn't know was possible. I look up into his eyes and they are heavy and hooded. He looks as though he's sad.

"What's wrong?" Did I say or do something to upset him? I couldn't have, I've said no more than a sentence. I take my hand from his and I stand. Confused, he looks up at me and watches me walk across the room to my stereo dock. I plug in my iPod. Music seems to be the gateway with this man and if I have a chance of him opening up to me, this might just do the trick.

"My choice this time," I say with a sly smile. I turn my back to him, but I can still feel his eyes on me. I scroll through my music collection and I settle on the first song that pops up: "Amaryllis," by Shinedown. The smooth opening of "stay a while now..." starts up, and I suppose it's fitting, because I really do want him to stay.

I turn around to find him staring at me, although this time I'm not fearful. Music has this effect on me; it's what gives me my confidence. Like how most people feel when they drink alcohol. "Can I get you anything to drink? I'm not sure how much I have." I walk to my fridge and open it, bending over to inspect the mostly bare shelves.

"I have Pepsi, cranberry juice, and a little wine left..." I have to stand to look at him so I can get an answer and when I do he's right there. He has got to stop doing that!

"I didn't mean to startle you," he says, his voice low.

"Yeah, you kind of say that a lot, you know?" I say with a huff.

"I'm sorry. I just don't know what to do or say around you, it's the craziest feeling. My gut says to try and get in your pants, but then I know that'll ruin whatever it is we have or may have. Then I get lost in my thoughts." Oh God, he rambles when he's nervous, too!

I just look at his gorgeous face and wait to see if he's finished. Well, he's stopped talking. He also dropped his head into his hands and now he looks a little lost. Frankly, so do I.

"Hey, I know exactly how you're feeling," I admit.

He looks down at me and waits for me to carry on. "I get it. OK, I am going to tell you something that I don't openly talk about and I hope it doesn't change the way you see me, not that I know how you see me, that is if you see me at all."

"I. See. You." He says each word slowly and individually. He's got my head in his hands and he's within kissing distance now. I freak and blurt it out, before it goes any further.

"I'm a virgin!" Yeah, that came out a little too forced. *God, kill me now.*

His sexy eyes widen and he takes a step back. *No wait, come back!*

He turns his back to me for a second before looking back at me. "What?" he asks in disbelief.

"I didn't mean for it to come out like that. Like I was assuming this was going to go any further, but you're the first guy that I have ever felt the need to tell and I know it came out all wrong and I am rambling again, I am so sorry." *Shut up.*

A new song comes on. He takes my hand and leads me to the little open space in the center of my studio. He twirls me. No one has ever danced with me and this song isn't exactly the slowest, but I'm not complaining. He pulls my body close to his, rests his right hand on my lower back and holds out his left for me to hold out from our bodies. And we begin to sway.

"So, all these paintings. Yours?" He gestures with his head toward the room around us.

I smile and I feel a blush take over my cheeks. "Yep."

"They are really nice." He presses a little tighter.

"Thank you."

He darts his eyes and throws his head towards one of my favorites. "This one, the stack of books I really like it. I take it you like to read?"

I nod slowly. "I do. It's my escape from this teeny apartment and small life."

He frowns a little. "Yes you do have a small place here, don't you? But I doubt your life is anything but small."

Before I can reply he notices something in the corner by my music station. He drops his grip on my lower back, which disappoints me a little. But he doesn't let go of my hand. Instead he's leading me over to his target in sight. What the hell does he see? He stops us in the corner and he's looking at the wall behind my dock and stacks of CDs.

Deep in thought, he looks from the wall to me. "These photos," he points to the wall. "You took them?" Oh, he noticed my slightly obscene collection of concert photos that I took...without permission...I know, I know, all the signs at every show say no cameras, but how can I resist? I love taking photographs of the musicians and the crowd. To capture that feeling in the moment; their high if you will. So if that means sticking my camera in my bra or down my pants, I'll do it! It's not like I can get one of those fancy "press" badges or "All Access" passes and bring my Canon into the venue. That's the dream.

"Yeah, I kinda had to sneak my camera into these places. My dream is to get in with my Canon, to get some really great shots," I admit.

His expression is soft and sexy as hell. "I think I have been to all of these shows."

I look up into his liquid caramel eyes. "Really? That's kind of a coincidence and I have never seen you at a single one."

He shrugs his shoulders and straightens his back. "That's because I go to the shows for work."

"Seriously?" I know my eyes must look like they are going to pop right out my little head; I am stunned and highly turned on.

"You know the music magazine *Tones*?" he asks.

I bolt to my coffee table, bend over to the shelf underneath and grab a stack of, like, ten magazines. “Uh, yeah! I do!” and I drop them next to my music dock.

He chuckles. “So I see where all of our Seattle sales have gone to.”

“So what do you do at *Tones* to get to cover shows?” I ask him with a bit too much excitement in my voice. *God, I must look like a preteen teeny bopper, fan-girling!* Breathe, Tess, just breathe.

He walks back over to the sofa and takes a seat. “I get to interview the rock bands. I have a column every month and each one is dedicated to one of the bands and shows. I get to review the setup, the crowd, and conduct an interview.”

Take me now! “Holy crap, that’s insanely awesome! Wait! No...no way are you THE Ben Mitchell!” Yup, I look pathetic...

“The one and only, babe,” he says with a wink.

Oh my, I think I just soaked my black panties. How can he turn me on with just a few words, and an eye movement?

He licks his lips. *I wanna do that...* “Look, I think I am avoiding why I came here tonight, why after seeing you in the class, and flipping out on you earlier...I am sorry again for that by the way.” And he’s still avoiding it...

“Ben, why are you here? And would you stop apologizing?”

He lets out a throaty moan. Oh my… "I want you. I want you so bad, it actually hurts. I am physically aching for you." His eyes are slits and he's leaning in closer to me.

I am too in shock to say anything. No man has ever come out and said that he wanted me before. They just typically get grabby. No, I don't want to think about that right now. I can't.

We make our way back to my red sofa. He puts his hand on my knee and starts to talk again, but all I can hear is the sound of my pulse in my ears. "Ben, I have never been so attracted to a man like I am to you. You don't know how confusing that is for me. My body is telling me to rip my clothes off and tear you out of yours, but my mind is telling me to take it slow." And honestly, I want my body to win this battle.

He nods his head. "I understand that, more than you know. I am used to fucking a girl and leaving right after. I haven't been on a real date since high school, for fuck's sake."

"But why are you telling me this? You just told me you wanted me and now you're telling me up front that you plan on 'fucking' me and leaving? How does that work out for you exactly?" I can feel my face getting hot with anger.

He shakes his head and throws his long fingers through his hair. "You don't get it. I want to take you out. I want to show you my place. I want to make love to you, NOT fuck you. You are more than just a fuck or any one-night stand."

Oh.

He brings his right hand up to my cheek and then his left. "Do you understand that?" I nod. "Good, because I am going to kiss you now, then I am going to stop, because I want to make damn sure you want me to do it again. There's no rush with us." I don't say a word.

He leans in slowly, watching for my reaction, I think. Maybe seeking my permission? He pulls away ever so slightly to look me in the eyes. I look back and then I close them. The next thing I know I feel his warm velvety lips on mine, moist from licking them out of frustration. Soft tender kisses. He begins to push a little more firmly, and I return with intensity. He must have liked it, because his hands are wrapped around the back of my head, in my hair. His lips part and I feel the tip of his tongue flick my top lip, enticing it to part with its bottom partner. I don't hesitate; I oblige by opening my mouth to him. He tastes like honey, sweet and smooth, just like his light accent. His tongue is exploring mine and my mouth sends a wave of heat down between my thighs. I grasp the back of his neck and pull slightly at his hair, and a low growl escapes his throat.

He pushes me down on my back, separating my legs with his knees. I can feel every hard inch of his toned body against mine. I feel how excited he is when he pushes a little harder at the apex of my thighs, making me even more excited. I want to feel him, I want to know how warm he is and how soft his skin is. I have never touched a man skin to skin in my life. I had no deep thriving desire to until I met Ben. Yes I was attracted to other guys in high school, but they didn't look at me twice let alone want to make out with me. No one wants the weird artsy nerdy girl. Except for this one guy...

Leaning over me, he whispers a plea, "Please tell me to stop. You're going to have to, if you don't want this to go any further. I know I said I would only kiss you tonight, but if you don't say stop I'm not going to."

I am not ready tonight, even though my body has a different agenda. I can't. This time I growl and he pushes his body harder between my thighs, and I grudgingly whisper, "Stop." *Nooooooooo!*

Closing his eyes, he slows our kissing. With one last soft peck, he drops his head.

"Thank you," he says, even though I half expected him to get upset. That's what every other guy did when I said to stop. "So, when you say virgin, how much 'virgin' are we talking about?" He winks.

I bashfully turn my head, and answer the embarrassing question, "*Virgin*, virgin." His eyes widen and his mouth drops open slightly. I can feel him beginning to get hard again. Oh this isn't going to be easy. To lighten the mood slightly I bite out, "And obviously you're not." I wiggle my hips beneath him.

"No, I am not, but if you keep on moving like that under me, you won't be for very much longer." But his tone isn't playful; it's stern and sexy as hell. Shit, if he were to try and get into my pants, I don't know if I'd have the willpower to say no. I just shake my head.

"Well, you are still on top of me," I finally reply, and he swiftly moves from the couch, holds out his hand, and helps me to my feet. Thank God, because my knees are so weak I would have probably fallen right on my face. He pulls me into a hug. Wow, this is nice and why does he have to smell so good? It's an oddly comforting smell and my heart twinges when I get this close to him.

"Hey"—he brings my attention up to his eyes, which stand over a foot taller than me—"what are you doing tomorrow night?"

I have to stop and think. I know there's something coming up. "I have plans tomorrow night," I answer.

He nods and lets out a little sigh. He actually looks a little sad. "OK. Well, how about I get your real number, so I don't have to keep trying to nail you through Chatz's chat room?" He pulls out his cell.

I read off my number as he punches it in, and then ten seconds later he calls mine. "There, now you have mine, call or text me any time. I am usually up late working on a project for work," he explains. "I will call you tomorrow afternoon, if that's OK?"

He's asking if he can call me, after he already got my number. "Uh, yeah, that's completely fine." I know I have a ridiculous smile on my face right now. *Play it cool, Tess.*

He leans down and plants another earth crumbling kiss on my mouth. I open my mouth first this time and a low moan escapes him. He pulls back and says, “Keep it up, I dare you.”

“Maybe I will,” I tease.

“Don’t.”

I back up a little and I walk him over to the door. “Uh, thanks for stopping by,” is all I spit out, like a moron.

He chuckles a little. “Yeah, sorry again about that, next time I’ll have your full permission.” And with that one little line, it feels like there’s a little something extra behind it.

He grabs his leather jacket and he’s out the door. Holy fuck.

Chapter Eight

~ Ben ~

I had no idea that SHE was going to be in Gwen's art class. I honestly didn't think I was going to see her again. How did I not notice her before in the class? Or even later at Chatz that night? But tonight, as she looks up at me from her spot at the table, ready to draw me in all my glory, I think I am going to come right here and now. Now this is something new. I have never in my whole life ever been so turned on just at the mere sight of a woman. OK, turned on, yes, but ready to bust a nut in front of a whole classroom is an entirely different thing here.

And now to have Gwen to ask me to stick around so she could finish my face ... I didn't know what I was going to say to do or say. Then the nerve of the woman, she leaves us. Alone. Don't get me wrong, I've wanted to be alone with this girl ever since I saw her at Chatz. I wanted her right then and there. But something inside of me says to leave her alone. She's not like any other woman I have wham-bam-thank you-ma'am'd. No, she is something more.

I can't help but notice that she is again having a difficult time looking at my face or in the eyes while she draws. I know I'm not bad-looking so that can't be it. I try to sit tight and not make her feel any more uncomfortable. Then she asks me if she can listen to some music. Huh, a girl who likes music just as much as I do, perhaps? I could get into this. I wonder what her taste is so I ask for a listen. I'm shocked when I heard Britney start to play and I want to play a little so I start to sing with it, just to see the look on her face. And boy, is she stunned. That's right, baby, you have no idea what I know.

When I ask to choose a song and I pick one of my favorites, that I haven't heard in a long time. Not too many girls I have been with have even heard of the band Good Charlotte. One point for Punky. But she takes the lyrics a little too literally and jumps down my throat, about how I must like girls who are like that. Oh, baby you can't expect to know me based on one song choice. I snap at her a little. Damn, why did I do that? How did this tight little body just get under my skin so fast?

She says she done and I want to believe her, but I have to wonder if it's because I have made her so uncomfortable. That's the last thing I want to do. She starts to pack up her belongings and she darts for the door right away. I can't let her get away without letting her know that I am interested. The next thing I know I am pinning her against the doorway.

By the way her breathing has gone heavy, I think she wants me too. But as soon as I give her an out she takes it. Any other woman would have been handing me their panties. But not her. She is beyond different, and I am intrigued. I need more. I need more of her.

So as I am pulling out of the campus on my bike I see that red-haired girl she was talking to at Chatz on Friday night, and a thought slaps me in the face, that maybe, just maybe she know where she lives. So, like the creeper I apparently am, I harass the girl until she gives up and has me follow her to Tess's place. *Harass* is a strong word, considering after the first ask she gives in...I don't know if that's a good or bad thing. On one hand, I didn't have to beg, but on the other, what if it was some other guy? Would she have given in so fast to escort him to her friend's house? God, I fucking hope not.

Once I finally got to her place, I take a deep breath before I knock on her apartment door, and I see Little Miss Trouble next to me giving me an odd little look and roll her eyes. *Uh yeah, I am fucking nervous, you don't know me, and you only saw what you want to see every week at Chatz.* So I knock and I hear her yelling from the other side of the door about a "him" in her class. She flings open the door. I swear I think all the color just rushed to and from her face in two seconds! Crap, I scared her! That's the last thing I wanted to do...way to go dude. And now she's off running into the bathroom. What the hell is she doing? I can't help but laugh, this is too good, and I am happy I did show up unannounced.

I have no trouble getting into the bathroom; she didn't even lock the door. Seriously, these two girls need to learn a thing or two about privacy and safety...not that I am complaining tonight. Considering it was their bad decisions that got me where I am right now.

I eventually get her out of the small bathroom. I hear her begging for her redheaded friend to stay. I have to step up and attempt to be polite, offer to come by or get together another time...and thankfully the girl catches my drift and hightails out the door.

Before we even start to talk, she looks like she's about to pass out. I am able to reach her before she hits her hard floor. I swiftly scoop her up in my arms and walk her over to her couch and lay her down. Wow, she looks really pale. When she comes to I tell her to eat something. And man, I am a fool for offering her a banana...watching her slowly put the fruit in her mouth makes me think dirty, very dirty things...

I take notice of all the artwork and I can understand her screen name at Chatz: Punky_Painter. She certainly has a lot of talent. I am trying to study a few of them as we dance in her small apartment. She has a lot of depth and personality in them. A little insight on how amazing I am sure she is. I hope I get to see more of that in her.

At home I think back to the remainder of the night. The evening progressed a little faster than I imagined it would. I can't believe she let me kiss her. Her body is small and tight. Her skin was soft and smelled amazing. The moment I ran my hand down he side and up her legs, she had chills. She even blushed at the most innocent touches and soft kisses. I can't remember the last time a woman blushed while I touched her. That's probably because they have been desensitized.

When she admitted that she really was a virgin, I just couldn't believe it. A young woman like her...I would imagine she could have any guy that she wanted. But I knew she wanted me. It took every thread in my body to not bend her over that red couch of hers. But I don't want a one-nighter with this girl. No, I want much, much, more, and that scares the crap out of me.

Chapter Nine

Tess

I decided to take the late morning/early afternoon shift at the coffee shop. I have tickets to see one of my favorite bands tonight, and I want enough time to grab a bite to eat and get ready before James, my older brother by two years, picks me up. James and I have always been close. He always looked out for me, which wasn't always easy, with me sneaking out to go to rock shows in high school and for my drastic "different" style choices I had made back then. I figured a guy wouldn't want to get with me if I looked more alternative, if I didn't look like the rest of the girls in my school, they'd leave me alone. So, since I was in the ninth grade, James took it upon himself to go to every show with me. Except for one.

I can't seem to shake my nerves from last night with Ben. First, he's a cocky bastard who turns stalker, sweet talker, then sexy mother effer. My mind and body are still playing catch up. Well I better start getting ready for work.

The morning is hectic with people getting an early start to their day, seeing that it's sunny for once in Seattle. People are out and about shopping and just hanging out. I see a lot more couples it seems like since my last shift...Dave, my partner in barista crime, can sense that something's up but he doesn't say anything. In fact, he's pretty quiet today. Odd. At times he almost seems truly pissed off at me. I have to wonder why. It never seemed to bother him that much when I turned him down to go clubbing or just to hang out. Maybe he's going through a breakup with one of his many boyfriends. I hope one day one of these guys will come in to see Dave, so I can see what his taste really is. I mean, all the other baristas boyfriends or girlfriends come to visit them at work. Huh.

As things start to slow by two o'clock, three hours till my shift ends, my phone rings. It's him! Get your crap together, girl! "Hello?" I answer.

"Hey, it's Ben..." He pauses.

"Yeah, I kinda got that when your name came up on my screen," I say coyly.

He lets out a slight sigh. "Yeah, I didn't think about that...so how's your day going?" he asks, sounding distraught.

Smiling like a fool, I say, "Pretty good, busy. I am at work right now, but I get off in a few hours."

He chuckles.

"What did I say?" I ask.

"Oh nothing, don't worry about it," he laughs.

Completely dumbfounded, I retrace my words...*oh my God!*

"Seriously?" I say a little louder than intended. "That you catch and find funny?"

"Hey, you said it, not me!" he defends himself.

Rolling my eyes, I say, "OK, OK, what do you want, other than to embarrass me in front of my co-workers and customers?"

"Oh baby, I could make you fall apart where you stand if I wanted to," he says matter-of-factly. And here come the heat waves.

I challenge him, "Oh, really? Is that so?" Yup, putting my big girl panties on. I walk to the back storage room.

He lets out a low growl. "Oh, you don't want me to do that while you're at work."

"I'm in the back room. Alone," I confess.

"Alone?" he asks.

"Uh huh," I nod my head.

"The things I want and will do to you..." He trails off. My knees go weak; I slip down to the floor with my back against a small row of metal lockers and bring them to my chest.

"When can I see you again?" he asks.

"Like I said, I have plans tonight, but tomorrow I am free. I have the day off of work."

His voice sounds a little more upbeat. "Call me when you get in tonight?"

"I am not sure when that will be," I tell him.

"Oh," and he's back to sad in a nanosecond. I cannot keep up, but he also doesn't need to know every inch of my life. I just met him, for cryin' out loud.

"Why don't you call me tomorrow afternoon?" I suggest.

"Sounds like a plan," he says, sounding a bit more chipper.

We say our goodbyes *hesitantly* on my end and I am back at the front counter getting death glares from Dave. *What?* I must have overshot my break...oops.

Three o'clock comes around and it's time to go home. Dave stops me in my tracks. "What was that all about earlier? Your head was in the clouds all morning, then you get this mysterious phone call, and now you're all googly-eyed."

"I'm sorry." I gather my belongings from the back room.

"You don't have to apologize, just wondering what's up with you the past few days, baby girl," he says, looking slightly worried.

I just glare at him, not really knowing what to say *I'm totally lusting over this nude model in my class in which he stalked my best friend and forced her to take him to my apartment, where we had an intense make-out session...* Yeah, I am thinking that might not come out sounding right.

"I'm good, really, don't worry about me," I say plainly.

"Mmm...hmm..." he says, clearly not believing me. "I'm going to ask again, like I always do, and maybe one day you'll say yes. Do you want to go out clubbing with me tonight? We can get all glammed up and hit the town, scout for hot boys." There is a beam of hope in his eyes.

I shake my head. "Not my kind of scene. I'd rather be home with my book boyfriend."

"I'll never get what you book sluts get out of a fictional man..." He shakes his head.

"Boys in books are better."

And that's that. I walk past him out of the back room, and out of the coffee shop, finally. It's been a long day with Ben on my mind, I just don't get him. As I am thinking about him yet again my back pocket buzzes. An incoming text from Ben: *Have a good time tonight...not too good of a time* ;)

I snort, ha! He actually used a winky face? I just shake my head, return my phone to my back pocket, hop in my car, and drive home. James will be here in an hour so I better get ready and force some food down my throat. I don't seem to be very hungry today, not with my thoughts returning to Ben and his body, the way his mouth tastes on mine...it's the only thing I seem to be craving. Ugh! I need a cold shower!

As punctual as ever, James is here right on time. I love that about my brother; at least one of us can show up on time. He knocks on my door and I rush to let him in. His six-foot frame towers over me he wraps me as up into a big bear hug. It's crazy how he got all the height, but we have different mothers. Before I was born, my dad had cheated on my mom for a while, and eventually he came clean. They got divorced, my mom got full custody of me, and mv dad ended up marrying his mistress.

I didn't find out that I had an older brother until I was about five years old. I started to have visits with my dad and his new family at that age. Up until that point I would cry about leaving my mom to go spend time with him because he was a total stranger to me. But once I met James we were attached at the hip. I started asking to go to my father's more often just so I could spend time with James. He was a cool big brother who didn't whine when I asked him to play Barbies or have tea parties. He wanted to make me happy. As I got older and began self-exploration, I found rock music and the feelings it provoked in me, the security and passion I felt then and still have now. I began to dress a little more alternative than the kids at my school, and that opened up the doors for bullies. Once James got wind of that, well, let's just say I didn't have any more problems at school. On the outside he looks like Kellen Lutz, a big ol' teddy bear in my eyes, but to someone who's about to receive a good beating. He's pretty damn intimidating.

I started going out at night to go to these rock shows alone, not having many friends, so alone was my only option. Mom didn't like the idea of rock concerts, and she hated the idea of me going to them by myself. So she put her foot down and said no altogether. I just went out my bedroom window.

I was about fifteen when I started doing that, and one night James was at the same small show I was, and he flipped out! Telling me how dangerous it was for a small young girl like me to be out alone at night, with drunken assholes all around me. The problem was that I didn't even notice anyone else when I was at a show. Once the music starts, I am consumed whole. So from that night on, whenever I wanted to go to a show he made me promise to take him along, for precaution. I love my big brother more than anyone.

"So are you ready, Tessy? Or do you need another half hour as usual?"

I stick my tongue out at him. "No, for once, I think I am good."

His eyebrows shoot up in shock. "Seriously? So does that mean we can head out a few minutes early and grab a bite to eat? I haven't had a chance yet, and I really fucking hate cheap venue food."

I grab my small black purse and my red Kodak easy shot camera and we walk out the door.

"So, where are you stashing that thing tonight? Or do I not want to know?" My brother only knows me too well. He knows that I will probably stick my camera in my bra to get past security. I'll be damned if I can't get any pics of this show! The band is freaking amazing!

"No, you don't," I tell him with a laugh.

He just drops his head and shakes it.

We decide to just do the whole drive-thru thing tonight since doors open in twenty minutes, and I like to rush to the front to get front and center to the action. The line isn't really all that bad, but I take notice that they are all wearing coats and will probably stop at coat check, ha! One step ahead! I didn't wear a jacket! Dumbasses. We get in and of course I am right, so I grab James's hand and run to the front of the stage. James takes his typical stance behind me to keep other fans from thrashing into me and to block any crowd surfers. He's my personal bodyguard.

The crowd really starts to pack in after the second opening act. With one arm at each of my sides, holding the barricade in front of us, James becomes my human shield. He never complains about doing this with me. One time I asked him and he told me he gets to see killer bands and shows, and spend time with his baby sister, even if that includes being slammed into and being dropped on. See why I love him so much?

The drummer beats his sticks above his head and the band jumps right into a hard fist-pounding song. And that's when my adrenaline kicks up a few notches. I begin to slam around and semi-head-bang. I am so not like the other girls at most of these shows. I don't come in wearing miniskirts and what look like bikini tops. I don't hop on shoulders and flash the bands. I am the girl in the jeans, Converse and a tank top. Simple. Clean and classic. I scream with the lyrics until I can no longer hear myself. I know I won't even be able to talk in the morning, but that's OK, because it's what I live for.

The band is halfway through their set and I reach into my top and pull out my camera while security is attending to a fistfight just left of the stage. But I'm being bumped into, and it's blurring my shots. If only I could be on the other side of this barricade with the other "press" photographers. One day, Tess. One day.

As I bob my head to one of my favorite slower songs, I see a great opportunity, so I whip out my little weapon and hold it out, only to find a figure right in front of me.

"You know you can't have that in here, don't you?" the tall figure asks.

It's Ben.

Chapter Ten

Tess

Oh. My. God. What is he doing here? And how is he in front of me? *Riiiight, he works for a music magazine dummy, you just talked about that.* But I was not expecting to see him here tonight. I actually haven't thought about him since I walked into this place. So to see him standing directly in front of me, at this moment, is blowing my mind.

He keeps eyeing me, waiting for me to say something, and then turns his attention above and behind me. That's when I remember that's where James is. Ben's eyes go from smoldering to ice cold. What is his deal?

"What are you doing here?" I ask him.

He looks back down at me. He has to speak up a lot more since the band has started a more upbeat song. "Work" is all he says.

Oh, this is how it's going to go down, is it? He's going to make assumptions? Well, guess what, buddy, you have no claims on me. We are not dating; I wouldn't even say we are friends. Just two people who have made out...

"Right, the magazine." I am not about to tell him that James is my big brother. Let him assume.

Talking even louder, he says, "Can I call you later after the show?"

Oh yeah, he's trying to make himself heard by James, trying to rile up some trouble, I am sure, or at least start a fight between James and I. I snort and roll my eyes at him.

"Text me" is all I say. And once more he looks from me to James, and he leans in and kisses me on the cheek, and nods.

OK, it was only a little kiss on the cheek, but that was all it took for me to reach my total high. I was there in my element: the music, the vibe from the fans, the heat in the venue, the scent that he was radiating in front of me, the smell of his sweet breath against my cheek. I am at a total loss. I can't control myself. The next thing I know I have my hands wrapped around the back of his neck, my fingers fisting the hair that grazes his neck, and I am pulling his mouth to mine. He didn't refuse me. Oh, thank god he didn't refuse me.

Pushing our bodies up against the metal barricade between us, he wraps his long toned arms around my waist. His tongue dips into my mouth and I can no longer hear or see anything but him. His tongue is hot, thrusting into my mouth with great force, and I think if he keeps kissing me like this I am going to come. And as much as I want that right about now, I don't want a venue full of people to witness it, let alone my older brother! SHIT! James is still behind me!

"Eh-hem," I hear come from behind me. I reluctantly pull away from Ben. His breathing is staggered and coming out harsh.

He licks his lips. "I'll call you later."

And he's gone. As he's walking back around the side of the stage, the band finishes their last song, everything begins to settle down and people start to leave the venue.

As James and I are walking out to the car, he speaks up. "Uh, you want to tell me what the fuck that was all about, Tess?"

I turn to face him "Oh, um...that was Ben." I shrug, trying to calm myself and not look like a little schoolgirl.

He eyes me and I can already sense his temper rising. Did I mention he's a very protective big brother? Oh crap, what am I going to say so that I don't sound like a slut, but to also to make sure he doesn't totally hate Ben?

"And who is 'Ben' exactly?" He's all macho.

Here we go. I suck in a big breath of cool Seattle air and tell him the story. Sort of. I end with: "So she left so we could talk. That's all."

His mouth has dropped open. "That's all? Are you sure?" He asks.

"Uh... yeah." I am not going to tell him about the make-out session.

"So, wait, you're seeing a guy who's a nude model?" He winces.

I can feel my cheeks heating up. "Uh, yeah..."

He throws his head back and laughs. “You really know how to pick ‘em, Tess.”

“What the hell is that supposed to mean, James? I haven’t even had a serious relationship with anyone, and you know that, of all people. Why I can’t.”

He throws his hand up in surrender. “You’re right, I’m sorry. I shouldn’t have said that, but really, Tess, a model?”

I roll my eyes. I know he didn’t mean to come off as so judgmental. “No, he’s not a model, he works at *Tones*, that killer music magazine that I am obsessed with. That’s why he was there tonight; he must be interviewing one of the bands there for a feature.”

The look on his face tells me something just clicked. “Wait, Ben Mitchell?” he asks me.

“Yeah, have you read his articles in the magazine?” I ask.

He bobbles his head from shoulder to shoulder. “Yeah, that, and I have heard he has quite the reputation when it comes to women, Tess.”

“Look, I’m not asking your opinion about the guy, I can take care of myself.”

“I know you didn’t ask for my opinion, sis, but you know I am always going to be defensive about you and anyone you might be seeing.”

I give him the tightest hug I could give. “I know and thank you, but please don’t worry. If I have an issue with him or any other guy I will let you know so you can introduce your fist to their face, OK?”

"You got it." He gives me a wicked grin.

Chapter Eleven

~ Ben ~

Who the hell was that guy with his arms around her sides tonight? Her boyfriend? She never mentioned anything about a boyfriend. Then again, I never did ask. She knows that I have a bad rep with the women at the bar, but fuck, I'm not seeing anyone. I haven't even slept with a girl since that night I first saw her. Granted I have had a lot of offers, I just don't want them.

Just thinking about her with that guy pisses me off. She says she's a virgin, so maybe it wasn't her boyfriend. He didn't try to stop me when she was sticking her tongue down MY throat. Ugh, just thinking about that kiss is making me hard. Fuck, it feels like forever since I did anything with a woman. Since meeting Tess, I find myself taking a lot of cold showers and reuniting my hand to my own dick. What am I, back in high school?

She told me to text her when I asked if I could call her, but I don't care. I need to talk to her. I need to hear her voice.

It's been two hours since the show ended, so if that were her boyfriend, then maybe he would be gone by now...I hope.

"Hello?" Her voice sounds sleepy.

"So, how did you enjoy the show?"

She lets out a soft yawn. How can a yawn sound so sexy? "I loved it. I love that band and being able to get up front was the most amazing thing ever."

Ever? "So not even our little public display of affection could top that?" I tease.

"Ha, I think it was a combination of both, actually." Her voice sounds a little more seductive now and I wish I were there. I picture her in a form-fitting tank top and panties on her bed.

"What are you wearing?"

She sighs. "Nothing special."

"Oh, come on, anything you wear would be special on you."

"My favorite T-shirt and boy shorts," she says, and my cock twitches.

A low growl escapes me. "Nice." And as much as I don't want to bring it up, I have to ask her.

"So, was that your boyfriend behind you tonight? If so how did he enjoy OUR little show?" OK, I know that sounded a little bitter, but I had to throw it out there.

She snorts. I can't believe she actually snorts, and she doesn't even try to cover it up like most girls would. "No.

That wasn't my boyfriend, Ben." Fuck, I love it when she says my name.

"Well then I hope it was a gay best friend or something, because I am not in the mood for competition with a straight guy friend who secretly has feelings for you, or whatever little teen drama show you have set up." OK, now I'm rambling, she's rubbing off on me. *hmm...that's sounds good right about now...*

"That was my brother James," she says.

Thank fucking God! I still have a chance with this girl. "Ah, that's good to know. I am surprised he didn't punch me for making out with his sister in front of a few hundred people."

"Nah, James is cool. He knows that if I need him to rectify a situation I'll let him know." She sounds like they're a Mafia family or something.

"Good, he should want to protect his amazing sister."

"Pfft" is all she lets out.

"When can I see you, Tess?" I'm in a hurry, but what can I say? I get excited around her.

I hear a wine bottle open when she replies, "Your call."

That's all it takes and I am on my way.

Chapter Twelve

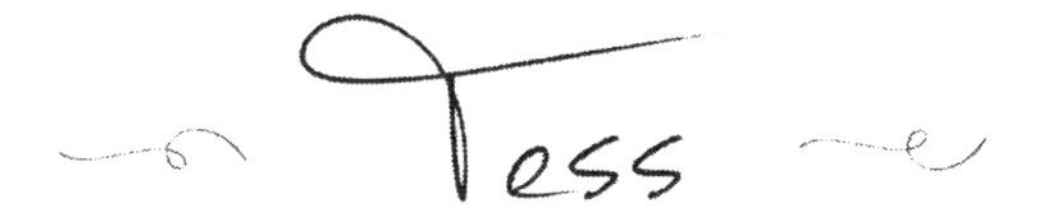

Frankly, I was hoping he'd call and want to come over. I want to get some answers about his so-called reputation. I know it's a little late, but I am wide awake, knowing he's on his way over here. SHIT! I better change. I don't want to be wearing my tiny shorts when he gets here! I run to my dresser and pull out a pair of black yoga pants and leave on my black T.

He must not live too far from me, because about ten minutes after we hung up, he's knocking at my door. I set down a half-drunk glass of wine that I had already poured to steady my nerves. Instead it's only making me horny, and knowing I am about to have Ben and his sweet ass and sexy accent filling my tiny apartment is not helping any. I open the door to see him holding a bouquet of flowers. Where on earth did he find a place open at this hour? And they are my favorite: peonies.

"Hi," I say when I meet his warm eyes.

"Hi," he replies. Scanning my body, he says, "Nice shirt."

He comes into the main room, takes off his black leather jacket, and lays it on the back of a chair.

"Have a seat. I'll pour you a glass."

He walks over to me instead. "Sounds great." He takes the bottle and pours his own glass and tops mine off. Taking my hand, he leads me to the sofa.

We talk about the wine, and I want to know what my favorite wine tastes like on his lips. But if I kiss him right now, I'll never get the answers I am looking for, but instead wake up in the morning no longer a virgin. I can't say no to this man. That excites me and terrifies me to my core.

I jump up and put my lovely pink plush peonies in a vase. From the kitchen, I speak.

"So, I hear you have quite the reputation with the ladies." I try to sound nonchalant.

He twists to look at me. "Now, who told you that?"

"My big brother says he's heard a thing or two." God, I hope he's not offended.

I walk back over and sit next to him on the couch. It feels impossible to keep a distance when we are in the same room together.

He takes my hand. "Look, I know your friend—what's her name, Erin?—has told you about the women I leave with at Chatz, but I can honestly say that since Friday night when I saw you there, I haven't been with a woman since."

I don't know if that makes me feel good or not. The fact that he has been with a lot of women worries me.

"How many women have you been with?" I take a large sip of my wine. Maybe that way when he tells me, I eventually forget by morning.

This time he shifts so his whole body is facing mine. "Does it really matter?" He asks me. I try to really think about that. I mean, it's in the past, right? You can't change how many people you sleep with.

"I guess not." I admit. I finish off my glass of wine. I stand to get another glass. "Refill?" I reach for his glass.

"Please." His smile is warm as he hands me his empty glass.

I stalk back into the kitchen, noticing that my legs are a little weak from the wine already. *Damn, I hate being such a lightweight.* As I fill our glasses I hear music coming from my stereo in the main room. I stop and see him setting his phone down next to my player with the cord connected to it.

He's playing his own music. He's got really great taste, from what I am hearing. I stare at his toned back, which is clearly visible through the thin white material of his tee. And in those jeans, his ass looks good enough to bite. He turns his head to see me in the kitchen, bends his arm, and crooks his index finger, inviting me to join him across the room.

I walk slowly to him. Taking in the soft melodic tune that he has chosen to play, my heart is beating a mile a minute. His hands go around my hips and he starts to sway with me. We slowly dance in the same spot, just holding one another. When the tempo picks up on the next song on his playlist, he takes my hand and twirls me around so my back is to his chest. Oh lord, he starts to move his hips into circles, with his finger in my hips he encourages me to follow suit. I circle and grind my backside to his front. I can feel the hardness of his chest at the back of my shoulders, along with the hardness at the lowest part of my back. Sending heat straight to my inner thighs. How can this man get me so riled up just from a few gyrations of his hips?

I lean my head back against his chest and he leans down close to my ear and whispers: "I need you. I crave you. You drive me wild. There is something different about you than any other woman I have ever met."

I let out a soft sigh and I just can't think. I don't want to think any more about him being with any other woman. I want to be with him. I want to be the woman he comes back to, and not be a one-night stand. But how do I truly know he can do that? Can I trust that he would stay true to me? I haven't known him long at all. We've never even been on a date. "But you barely know me Ben and I barely know you."

He nods slowly understanding. "What do you want to know?" He asks me.

What do I want to know? I want to know everything, but where to start. It's like one of those things when you walk into a music store and you want to pick up some new music, but your mind goes blank on what band you wanted to look for. I just stare at him for a moment. Ben chimes in, "Why are you still a virgin? How did I manage to find most likely what is to be the last and final one in the city?"

Ha. He would have to bring this up. I shake my nerves and start to talk. "He was a couple grades above me. He gave me my first kiss, but then quickly tried to grope me and I wasn't ready. So when I told him "no" he didn't stop. He kept trying to force himself on top of me, by shifting his body across the bench seat of his pick-up truck and pinning me. My shoulders and head up against the cold glass window and his hands were running up my thighs to my breasts. I decided it was now or never and I swiftly brought my leg up just enough to nail him right in his sack." Ben winced at this part of my flash back.

"He coiled back, called me a "fucking bitch" and a "tease." I took the opening and bolted out of the truck and he drove off..." A tear runs down my cheek. I never spoke about this with anyone, but I feel like I can tell Ben anything. If all else fails at least I can say I opened myself up to him.

Ben wipes my tear and wraps an arm around my waist. "You don't have to tell me anymore if it hurts Tess. I understand."

Needing to finish my story not only for Ben but for myself, I go on. "No. I need to tell you everything...He abandoned me in the parking lot at a local park, at night, leaving me to walk five miles home. After that night I didn't go out on any dates. I stayed home on weekends, cranking my tunes and painting."

Ben gently kisses me on my forehead, "Thank you for telling me this. I am sorry you had to go through something like that."

I huff, if he only knew half of what I've been through...

"So, what about you Mr. Man Whore? Why all the women?" I ask. *Hey if we're being honest here.*

Rolling his eyes at my name calling, he starts in. "Well after being in a serious relationship for far too long with the wrong person, I may have taken the rebound phase a little too serious and kept rebounding."

"Sounds more like re-mounting" I say with a snicker. *Yep too much alcohol for Tess...*

Before I can say anything he continues. "I am not asking to sleep with you tonight. I am only asking that you become mine."

What the hell does that mean? "Yours?"

"Mine. I want to know that you won't go on any dates with any men. That you won't give yourself to them. I want that. I want to be worthy of being your first."

Oh.

I huff out, "You're not the one who needs to worry about that. You're the man-slut who can take home a different girl, every night or two a night." OK, that may have sounded harsh, but seriously, does he really think he has that right to ask me not to sleep with a guy? Considering I have NEVER slept with a guy?

At this point we are facing one another completely. No distance between our bodies. "I know I don't have a right to ask this of you, but I promise the same to you. I will not sleep with anyone. I will not take a woman on a date."

OK, that makes me feel slightly better. "What do you want to do then?" I ask.

"I want to take this as slow as you need to. I want you to trust me." He looks desperate. Why does this mean so much to him?

"Why though? You can go out and sleep with any woman. Who's to say I'm going to sleep with you? What if I said I was saving myself for marriage?" I test him.

His mouth pops open and he takes a moment to think about it... *yeah I thought so, I'm not sounding so great, now, am I? Not if I'm talking about marriage and waiting to have sex...*

"Uh huh! See!" I screech out. "There's no way you could wait that long!"

He grabs the sides of my face with his hands. "I would wait for you." He is serious. I can tell. Wow.

"Just so you know, I'm not waiting till I get married." I confess.

He gives me that killer sexy grin and says, "I don't want to say that I am relieved, but on some level I am, because I don't have a ring to give you right now." *What?*

I snort. "Whatever."

"I meant what I said. You would be worth the wait." He kisses me softly.

As we begin to kiss lightly I pull away slightly, I look into his eyes and I can feel the heat rising in my cheeks before I even say the words. "I'm not against other things in the meantime."

A low growl to which I have become accustomed returns from deep inside his throat. He pushes his forehead into the crook of my neck and shoulder. "You're going to kill me, you know that? Keep saying things like that and I will take you to your bed."

I take his hand and lead him to my queen-sized bed. Looking up into his warm eyes, I grab the hem of his shirt and pull it up over his head. I run my hands over his lean toned abs, but he grabs them and brings them up to his mouth and kisses my knuckles lightly.

"We don't have to do anything you're not comfortable with. What is the most you have done?" he asks, but it doesn't offend me, which shocks me.

I shrug and look at our feet. "Nothing."

He lifts my chin with his hand and looks at me for a long moment. In his smooth-as-silk accent, he says, "Then I want to be the one to make you come first."

He takes my mouth with his passionately, exploring every nook of my mouth, and I can feel my knees shaking. No man has ever touched me. Anywhere. He runs his hands down my shoulders, my ribs, and rests them on my hips. He reaches around to my backside and I can feel him getting hard again. He's kissing my neck, down to the dip in my throat. I am holding onto his biceps for dear life. I feel like I am going to collapse at any moment. As if he can read my mind, he backs me up to the edge of my bed and lowers me slowly. I am on my back when he stands up and looks over my body. I have never felt so exposed.

I nod, knowing he's asking permission with his eyes to remove my fitted pants. He leans between my legs, I lift my hips, allowing him to slip his fingers beneath the waistband and pull them down over my backside, down to my knees, and off my body. He gasps when he sees my baby blue lace panties. He adjusts himself from the outside of his jeans. He looks almost uncomfortable. I sit up quickly and I startle him by the look on his face. I reach for the button of his jeans. He eyes me wearily, and stops me. He steps back, undoes the button, and slowly lowers the zipper. He's wearing black fitted boxer briefs and I can see his erection much more clearly now.

Wow.

Ben leans down and slowly raises the bottom of my black tee up over my belly and my small chest, up over my head. I didn't even realize that I didn't have a bra on...oops.

He lays me back on to my bed, tracing soft kisses from neck, down to my heaving chest. No one has been this close to me. The next thing I know he has my right nipple in his mouth, swirling his tongue around the sensitive mound. A moan escapes me and I bite my lip to prevent another one to come out.

"Don't hide from me, baby. I want to hear you. I want to know that I am the one pleasing you. The first one." And so I do. I let out another soft moan as he makes his way to the left. I plunge my hands into his dark hair and pull. With that he groans and pushes his concealed length against the soft tissue at the apex of my thighs. Holy crap, this is amazing. I can't even imagine how good it's going to feel when he's actually inside of me.

I tease him back and raise my hips to meet his. He bites down a little on my nipple and I almost scream.

"Oh, not yet baby. I'm not going to make you come like this...well, not tonight." He talks in a breathy tone. I can feel myself getting wetter and wetter. He reaches down to my panties and slips them off in one swift motion. I am completely bare before him now. He lowers his body to my bed, kissing a trail from my belly button to my hips, where he gives me a little nip and I let out a small giggle.

"Ticklish, are we?" His grin is sly.

He continues his journey down my body. To my knee, then down my calf. Thank god I shaved my legs this morning. To my ankle, and he licks my instep of my foot. He then repeats this trail back up the right leg before stopping at the core of my lower body. He flashes me a little grin and bows down to lick the slick flesh of my folds.

Oh. Oh my.

"You taste so sweet. And you're so wet for me. I want you to come for me, so relax, because I am going to take care of you." And with those last few words I fall for him. Because I know that when he says that he's going to take care of me, he means more than just pleasuring me.

He goes slowly at first, circling and circling. I am involuntarily moving my hips to his tongue. It's as if I have no control over my own body. As my panting becomes more rampant, he starts to suck on my clit. I begin to tense up and my body starts to shake. I can feel the build, and then he nips at me, and that's all it takes. I come around his face. My body is shattering and I don't want this to end.

"That's my girl." He begins to slow his pace, letting me come down.

I am his.

Chapter Thirteen

I didn't see Ben for the next couple of days. But he texted me often and called at night. He's been really busy at work; apparently he's really working on this huge piece for the magazine. Which is all right with me, because Dave asked me to cover for him tonight at the coffee shop, which means I'm pulling a double shift. I can use all the extra cash I can get. The late-night customers like to tip big. I think they like to show off to their dates proving they have money. I'm not complaining.

It's almost eleven o'clock and I'm wiping the counters down and re-stocking the mugs for the morning shift, about to close, when I get a text from Ben: *So where is it that you work anyways?*

I tell him, and he replies: *OK, well, have a good night. Call me in the morning x.* Oh, I'll have a good night thinking about him, and what we did the other night, and all the things I hope to do to him in the very near future.

Almost instantly after, my phone rings, I look at the caller ID; it's Erin.

"Where have you been? It's like you dropped off the grid or something!" She sounds exasperated.

"I am sorry. I have been...occupied." I can feel my cheeks go pink instantly.

"OH? What could be more important than calling your new best friend, huh?" She's trying to sound wounded, but instead I can hear the intrigue in her voice.

"Uh, yeah...I have been working and I went to this show with my brother...and got together with Ben..." I trail off.

"BEN? I knew it!" She is screaming at me, actually screaming, right now.

I'm rubbing my forehead with the left hand, just taking it all in. "Why didn't you call me? Text me? Anything!"

"I am so sorry, but I am trying to comprehend all of this myself."

She grumbles. "Meet me at Chatz in ten minutes. I know where you work and I will come kidnap you if I have to!"

Fifteen minutes later, I spot Erin in the far corner, where there is a grouping of deep purple sofas facing one another. She is chatting it up with a beefy blond guy in a three-piece suit; he obviously just left work himself. She looks up and greets me with a hug.

Erin introduces me to the beefcake. "Mark is an ad exec at Pillars Advertising." She spews lust as she says the words.

"Impressive." I try to sound intrigued, but I honestly don't give a shit. I am tired and cranky from a long day and night at work. But I will stay for one drink and make my way home.

When I reach the bar I see a small dark nook at the end. There's a blonde woman looking quite comfy on a man's lap. They aren't kissing, but she is obviously trying to nuzzle the man's neck. As I reach for my drink, they stand. And my heart sinks. The leggy blonde is leading Ben towards the door. My way.

Fuck! What the hell do I do? Confront the man who I was intimate with just over forty-eight hours ago? Or do I hide like a shamed little girl? I take a large chug from my drink, which sparks a howl from the bartender, obviously impressed. And that brought some looks my way. Well, if I had a chance of backing down before, I definitely don't now. Shit.

I stiffen my back and face the oncoming pair, face first. And the look on his face is fucking priceless.

"Tess!" he gasps.

Son of a bitch. "Ben."

"Um, what are you doing here? Didn't you just get off work? I figured you'd be home by now." He sounds nervous, as he should be.

Not that it's any of his business, but: "Erin called me after you texted me and begged me to come tonight."

He looks into the lounge and nods when he spots Erin. She is still talking up the beefcake. He looks back at the leggy blonde, who has her slutty hand holding his arm. "This is Nicole."

He looks me dead in the eyes like he's trying to tell me something, but I must be missing something, that or the rum I just downed is killing my brain's cells at record pace. He's never spoken about a girl by name before so I am not getting this little message he's trying to send me.

"Hi." I say, trying not to give her the look of death. I don't know why I am so angry. It's not like he's mine. But then again he asked me to be his...yeah, which number on the list? Then I am brought back to our conversation the other night, how he wants me to trust him. *Well, buddy, you have a fat chance in hell of that happening now.* And that hurts me. It hurts real bad. I was beginning to trust him.

"Would you mind giving me a minute?" he asks the bimbo.

She nods, and tries to kiss him, but he turns his face away avoiding her cotton candy glittery lips. She looks pissed and not so much at him, but me, because as soon as he dodged her glossy pucker she eyes me and looks back to Ben. "Yeah, whatever. Don't take too long."

Then she's off toward the restroom.

"What the fuck?" I spurt out before he can speak. He has to know I am pissed and that he better protect those family jewels, because they are about to meet the top of my kneecap.

He reaches out to touch my cheek, and this time I dodge him. “I can explain,” he pleads. Yeah, I have heard that so many times in so many movies. He’s about to tell me that she’s the love of his life that got away and has suddenly returned, and his heart has been and will always be with her. OK, maybe I shouldn’t watch so many movies or the CW...

“Then explain.”

He shifts on his feet. “Not here. Will you come back to my place with me?” Now, that I did not expect to come out of his sexy mouth.

“What about ‘Nicole’?” I mimic his light English accent. Yep, too much rum, too fast.

He steps closer. “What about her?”

As I am about to talk he takes a small sidestep to get the attention of the bartender. “You’re just going to leave without a word?” I wait. Why am I being thoughtful of the skeez?

He leans in over the bar to tell the bartender something, so I wait.

“I left a message for her with Ron there,” he says, while grabbing my elbow and leading me toward the doors. *Shit! Erin!*

“Hold on! I have to tell Erin that I am leaving or she’ll worry.”

He looks back at where Erin is sitting “I don’t think so.” He says and shoots his chin in her direction. I look over and she’s practically straddling the beefcake.

“OK” I say, and he leads me out of the bar.

When we get outside, I whip out my cell and text Erin a quick message: *Something came up have to go, I'll call you in the morning*. Ben leads me to the back parking lot of Chatz. Which car is his?

Oh, you have got to be kidding me.

"Of course you drive a motorcycle," I say.

He grins, and my insides melt. *NO! You cannot make me fall apart like this! Not after what I saw you and that bimbo were doing in that dark corner!* He hands me a helmet. *Oh, here we go, what am I getting myself into?* I take it from his hands and our fingertips touch and I can feel that spark of intensity. Still trying to be angry, I take the helmet from his hand a little too hard and accidentally kinda throw it to the ground. *Yeah, that's the way to look tough Tess...*

Laughing, he bends down to pick up the helmet, and yes, I'll admit I checked out his ass. What's wrong with me? Fucking rum. This time, instead of handing me the helmet, he places it on my head gently. He throws one on his head next and throws down the visor, swings his right leg over the black seat, holds out one arm. "Get on," he demands, with a little force.

I roll my eyes and get on the bike behind him. I have never been on a bike before. I am nervous and yet excited to have to sit so close to him. I try to resist and sit as far back as I can. I lightly hold his ribs. When he kicks on the machine, the vibrations make me all tingly between my legs and I am not complaining! He reaches down with both hands grips the back of my knees and pulls me in closer behind him. That, mixed with the shaking between my thighs, makes me think I might come right then and there.

"That's better." He kicks into gear and soon we are speeding through the lighted city. I can feel my nails digging into his chest, but that doesn't seem to slow his speed; hell, I'd say it's probably turning him on. Soon, we're in a parking garage, and he's

leading me to an elevator. He presses the top floor button: '*PH*' for penthouse. Of course he lives in the penthouse.

A moment later we're inside.

Whoa. For a dude's place this is pretty damn nice. Much, MUCH, nicer than my tiny studio. We walk in through the small foyer to an open floor plan studio suite. Tall ceilings and a wall of windows, overlooking the Seattle skyline. His walls are all different colors: white, deep red, and a single black wall holding a collection of guitars and basses.

He offers me a drink. I decline. He shrugs and gets a beer. I'm impatient.

"So you wanted to explain. Explain." I gesture with my hand to urge him on.

He looks ashamed. "I know it's not a good excuse, but I was pretty buzzed and kinda-sorta horny from our texts all day and I was having a hard time shoving her off."

What an ass. "If I wasn't there, would you have brought her here or went to her place?" I say with as much force as I can push, but my breath is taken away from me. I am actually holding back some tears. No. I will not cry about a guy I know nothing about. Not shed a tear for a man who has probably slept with every woman in Seattle.

He looks down at his feet and lifts his eyes to mine. "No."

"Yeah, I bet!" I yell.

"I mean it, Tess. I wasn't going to go anywhere with her. I was leading her out to her car when I saw you."

"But, you two looked nice and cozy in that corner and she was holding your arm when you were walking out, I don't know about you, but I am pretty sure a girl that looks like that doesn't take rejection very well." I know I sound snide.

He runs his hands through his midnight hair and that's all I want to be doing right now. Yes, despite what's taking place right now. My body seems to have a mind of its own lately. "So let me get this straight, this girl that means nothing to you jumps you in a bar and you let her kiss your neck and then you are able to escort her out without a single lash-out from the bimbo?"

Oops that slipped out...

His eyebrows shoot straight up. "Bimbo?" he asks with a grin.

"Yes. Bim-Bo." I enunciate each syllable.

He looks impressed now. Why?

"Well, she is one." He laughs. "Look, I do know her, but it's not what you think at all."

"I honestly don't know what to think right now, Ben. You're going to have to fill me in here or I am walking out of that door."

"It's not really a story I can tell without telling you a little more about myself first." He pauses, considering his next words. "Which is something I don't do with anyone. I figure it's no one's business." He says sternly and shuts off. He stops and thinks for another moment. I can feel some tension.

"I first moved here from London with my father and baby sister when I was fifteen." He's opening up to me.

"My mum had died when I was ten. She passed away giving birth to my baby sister Caroline." He swallows hard, and I can tell he's reliving the crushing scene in his mind.

"My mum was an amazing woman. My dad cherished her and treated her like the queen she was. She was a classic beauty, kind and fair. She always smelled like flowers. She loved to garden so she spent a lot of time out in the yard. She had me out there helping her all the time. I didn't care if it wasn't the normal 'boy' thing to do, I loved my mum and any time spent with her was great." He's smiling at the sweet memory.

"But, what I think hurt the most was that Caroline would never know our mother the way I was able to. She wasn't going to have a mum to look up to. To play dress up or have tea parties. No mother to teach her how to wear makeup and just about being a young lady." I can see tears begin to fill his eyes, and I can't keep my own from shedding. He reaches up and wipes my tears with his thumbs, caressing my face.

"I have always looked out for my baby sister. She is my whole world." He chuckles. "Hell, I even played dolls with her and tried to fill in for my mom as much as I could.

"My father was offered a job here in Seattle shortly after my mother's death. We all agreed that a fresh start would be ideal. So he took the job and here we are."

I finally speak up. "And what does that have to do with what I saw at the bar?" His story touches my heart, it really does, but I need to know why he can demand I be *his,* and yet I catch him with another woman.

Looking up from his dropped head, he looks me in the eyes. "Look, she isn't anything to me. Only a part of my past I want to forget. She came in looking for, after I sent her an email telling her I didn't want to hear from her again. I am sorry you had to see that. She's just persistent."

"One of your one night stands?" I hiss out.

"No."

Sensing his anger, I watch what I say. I think for a moment. "Just tell me this then. When we spoke the other night you mentioned that you didn't until as of more recently started man slutting. Is she one of the reasons why you lost it?"

He nods. His eyes begging me to drop it and I will...for now. "You were saying about your family?" I ask, trying to calm him back down.

Ben shakes his head. "So, my dad, he told my sister and me that no one could ever compare to our mother. He has dated a few women. Honestly, I think he just dates them to try and fill some empty void. He never gets too close."

"You said you've never talked about this with anyone. Why me?"

He looks me in the eye. "There's just something about you, Tess. I feel like I can tell you anything and you won't turn around and spread my business or use it against me. That's also why I brought you here, to show you."

"What does that mean?" I ask.

He waves his hand. "I have never brought anyone here other than my father and sister."

Oh.

I can feel my cheeks go red. "Why, though? You seem to be such a private person and you haven't known me for more than a week."

He takes my hands and brings them to his mouth. Kisses my knuckles softly and I can see the gears in his head turning.

"What it is? I can see that you're thinking about something."

"I don't know if it's appropriate." He looks uneasy.

I give him a little coy smile. "Ben, when have you been appropriate with me?"

He smiles that panty-dropping smile that I first saw, that first night at Chatz. "It's just a personal question that I want to ask. And I don't want to turn you off."

OK, that's not going to happen. "That's just not possible, Ben. You could never turn me off."

He closes his eyes for a second and a low deep sensual groan escapes his slightly parted lips. "Tess," he says, and with that one word, that one breath, I feel my panties getting moist.

I bit my bottom lip, holding back my own groan. "Ask me whatever you want Ben."

He exhales in a rush and straightens his body so he's facing me completely. "Do you touch yourself, Tess?" WHOA! Where did that come from? He said personal, but that, that's *personal...*

My cheeks flush and I drop my head. I have never spoken about sex with anyone, not even my own mother. It wasn't a normal thing to talk about. I didn't even have any girlfriends in high school to talk to about this stuff. Only Erin, and I just met her the same time I met Ben. Now that girl is a horn-dog.

"Why do you want to know?"

He leans in closer and places his mouth closer to my ear. I can feel his ragged breath and I almost jump when he whispers, "Because I am hoping to be the first and *only* person inside of you."

Oh god. I am going spontaneously combust.

"So, have you or have you not, ever put your fingers inside of yourself?" he has no shame.

I can't even think. My head is spinning from his words. All I can get out is a barely audible "no."

And then his mouth is on mine. Hot. Hard and needy. I reach up and twist my fingers through his hair, trying to pull him closer, but I can't seem to get close enough.

Fuck this!

I push his chest back until he fumbles onto his black leather couch. I throw one leg over his lap and I straddle him. My chest heaves with uneven breathes. He holds my hips for a few moments and runs then up my ribs, then back down to reach up under my shirt. He undoes my bra, then lifts my shirt over my head. Before I can even lean forward to keep kissing his amazing mouth, it's on my left breast. He kisses it at first, then licks the tip of my nipple, and I can't help but moan...loudly. I can feel his smile against the skin of my breast. With that he stands, but keeps my legs wrapped around his waist. He starts kissing my neck as he lifts me up and carries me past the kitchen and heads down the small hallway I noticed before. He kicks open a door and walks in backwards.

He lays me down on what I am assuming is a bed and stands in front of me, eyeing me. I can't stop looking at him. He removes his own shirt, to reveal his slim toned shoulders and chest, and I can see the magnificent tattoos that cover his whole arm. He starts to undo the button on his jeans.

"Don't worry, I won't do anything you don't want me to. All you have to do is say stop and I will." I know I can trust him. I don't know how, but I can. And trust doesn't come easy for me.

I give him a little nod and he continues to unzip his pants. He hooks his thumbs into the waistband and slowly starts to pull them down, leaving his boxers. He drops them to the floor and steps out of them. He surely is a glorious sight.

He grabs the back of my knees and pulls me to the edge of the bed. He begins to undo the buttons of my jeans. He doesn't stop to seek permission, because we have made it this far before. He rids me of my pants and panties in one shot. I am now completely naked. Feeling brave, I sit up right in front of him, inches away from his concealed arousal. I lick my lips and I reach forward for his shorts. He takes a tiny step back, which shocks me.

"What?" I ask him.

He sighs. "If I let you touch me, I will go mad."

Oh, that's hot.

I once again reach for his shorts and he sucks in a tight breath. Careful not to touch his erection, I pull them down slowly. I watch his eyes the whole time and he looks down into mine. I can see his desire for me; it makes me feel brave. I stare at his intimidating size.

Amusement is in his voice. "Don't worry. When the time comes, it won't be as bad as you think." He makes it sound like I am a porcelain doll and he's afraid of breaking me. Well, news flash. *I am tougher than you think.*

"Oh I don't think it'll be bad. I know it'll be amazing, and remember, I have already seen it." I wink.

"Then maybe I'll enforce a no-touching policy then?"

"Well, I would break all the rules, then." I retort, then mouth "*rebel*" while pointing at myself. I reach out for him and before he can move away I have my hand wrapped around his stone-hard length. His groan is almost a growl. At first it sounds almost like he's angry. I can feel the vibrations from his tone go right between my legs. He grabs my wrist and pulls me up.

"What did I say would happen if you touched me?" he growls. Holy crap. Should I be turned on or should I be scared?

He runs his right hand down my ribs, then to my hips and stops below my belly button. Less than an inch away. "Spread your legs," he orders. And I do it.

He moves his hand between my fold and slides over my slick clit. Rubbing me gently, he nips at my neck, and then he's laying me back down on to his bed. He lays to my left and keeps rubbing me. I can feel my body start to tense and then he stops. WHY?

I let out a soft whimper.

"That's just for starters, baby," he whispers. "I want to be your first. It's all I can think about since you told me you were a virgin." I reach again for his erection, and this time he doesn't pull away. For the first time, I stroke a penis. It's hard and smooth, almost velvety. I start to move a little faster and he groans again. His eyes shoot open and he once again grabs my wrist.

"Fuck. I have never been so close so quick. What is it about you?" He sounds bewildered.

I shrug and give a small smile.

"Oh, baby, I am nowhere near ready to end this so quickly." And he reaches between my legs and my body floods with excitement as his fingers pass my small mound, and he's at my opening. My chest starts to pound, nervous and excited all at once. He looks into my eyes, and I nudge my hips up to meet his fingers and he slips one inside.

Holy...

No pain, just all sensation. He slowly goes in and out, making me wetter as he does. And he gradually introduces a second finger, and that's all it takes. I am convulsing with pleasure. He keeps up his pace while going in and out, then with his thumb presses on my clit. Heaving for a deep breath I begin to let down. And then he pulls out. He licks his fingers. I blush and look away.

"Does that bother you?" he asks softly.

"I don't know. It's just odd for me, that's all. All of this is so new for me."

He nods his head and lies next to me. "Oh, it gets better. So much better."

"I thought that was pretty fucking amazing." He laughs. Then a thought occurs to me. "What about you? This is the second time you haven't gotten anything." Feeling guilty.

"I want to please you, and by doing so it pleases me. You don't have to worry," he tells me, but I have to wonder: If he's not getting it from me, then is he getting it somewhere else?

"But you have needs, and this cannot be enough for you. Do you see someone else after you leave me?" I am afraid of his answer.

"No. No Tess, you're the one I want to be with, even if that means a cold shower after we part ways, or a solo job." And I get all hot again, just imagining him in the shower, pumping himself. And then I get a little brave again...

"Do you think about me?" I can't believe I just asked that. But, hey, I want to know.

"Yes." He breathes.

Oh. My.

I wake up in Ben's bed. I look around for a clock; it's after three o'clock in the morning. I roll over to see if Ben was asleep, but he wasn't there. I sit up, wrap the black sheet around me, and head out to the main living area. The room is dimly lit, by the city lights beaming through the large windows. I find him sitting on the sectional with his back to me, holding what looks like a bass guitar. His back is bare and all of his muscles look defined from the way he's holding the bass. He has it plugged into a small amp and the volume is down so low I can barely hear it from the hallway. I quietly tiptoe over to him, not wanting to mess him up or startle him. He's playing a slow tune, nothing I recognize. I walk around one side of the sofa and sit down next to him. He looks over to me and smiles, but doesn't stop playing.

"Did I wake you?" he asks.

"No, I woke up probably knowing I wasn't in my own bed." He nods and smiles.

"Not too many people play the bass. Most want to play the cool guitar." I wink.

"Well, I make the bass look cool."

"No, more like dreamy and sexy as hell."

He sets the bass down and that's when I notice that he has his black boxer briefs back on. Bummer.

He strides to the kitchen. "Are you hungry?"

My stomach growls, giving me away.

He smiles and reaches into the fridge. Pulls out a few different Tupperware containers, filled with God knows what. "OK, I have spaghetti and meatballs, baked chicken, roasted garlic potatoes and vegetable lasagna." He lists off.

"Vegetable lasagna, please, and did you cook all of this yourself?" Nothing is sexier than a man who can cook.

He looks proud. "Yep. With mom gone and dad at work most nights, it was either Maria the maid slash nanny slash cook, which all she knew was mac 'n' cheese or how to dial a phone for takeout. So I learned how to cook. Really wasn't that hard. Added bonus that I learned I enjoyed it too."

He throws the container in the microwave, then grabs a bottle of wine and two stem glasses. "Do you like Moscato?"

"It's my favorite, actually." I take a small sip, of the cold refreshing liquid. I lick my lips to savor it, and I notice Ben watching me intently with thumb at his mouth nibbling the tip. Hot.

Moments later, he dishes out the food, and sits next to me at the breakfast bar. "So, I told you about my family drama. What's your story?"

"Not much of one," I begin. "Dad cheated on my mom when I was a baby, they got divorced. He married the other woman, and years later we found out he already had a son with her. Hence the brother you 'met' at the show. Mom raised me alone with little help from my dad, never knew I had a brother for a while. When we did meet, we became inseparable."

Ben nods that he understands, and I know he does. I know what Caroline means to him. I go on. "I went to school, shows, painted, taught myself how to use a camera. Got a job at the coffee shop after high school, took a few years off, saved up some money, and am now taking a few classes over at the community college, which you know."

He stares at me, wide-eyed. Ha!

"See, not so exciting," I say.

"It's your life. It's exciting to me." Wow, he knows how to lay it on thick.

We finish our meal and I get dressed. I ask him to take me home, because I have a late morning shift at the coffee shop. Ben excuses himself to take a quick shower. Oh, how I'd love to jump him in there one day. I take a closer look at the wall I noticed last night. The one covered on guitars and basses. As I look closer, they are all autographed! And by some of my favorite bands: Good Charlotte, Maroon 5, Shinedown, Three Days Grace and a whole lot freaking more! He comes up behind me and wraps his arms around my waist.

"These are amazing!" I burst out.

"I'm glad they impress you."

"You impress me, Ben." I lean my head and look up at him. Yeah, he's smiling too.

"Well, if you aren't busy tomorrow night, I am covering the Maroon 5 show and, well, I can easily get an extra pass..."

Before he can even finish, I screech, "YES!" and I literally jump up and down with excitement. I don't care how lame I look right now!

He is full-on laughing right now, and his hefty laugh is intoxicating with his accent. Oh my...

"Well, I see that you are excited, but there's one more little thing."

"What?" I drag out the word.

"You bring your Canon."

I scream. I let out the most ear-piercing fan girl scream. “Seriously?” I look at him, wide-eyed.

“Seriously, I know you want to use a good camera at a show for once. And being with me you can get up close and personal.” He explains.

Oh. I am. In. love.

Chapter Fourteen

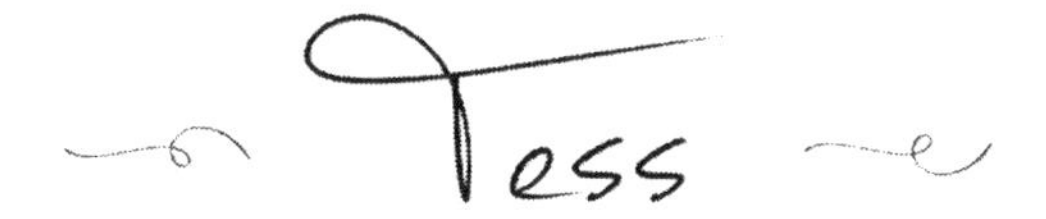

"Hey, since you threw me on your bike last night, I need to be taken back to Chatz to pick up my car."

He runs his left hand through his glorious midnight hair, gives me a sly smile. "Yeah, I would say sorry about that, but I'm really not."

I just shake my head and start out of his place. When we get back to the bars parking lot it's empty. Not something I am used to seeing at Chatz, but then again it is early morning. Ben jumps off his bike and helps me off of the mean machine, my legs still shaking from the violent vibrations, that and squeezing Ben between my thighs.

We walk over to my little red baby. I stop and lean my back against the door. Ben reaches forward and tucks my hair behind my ears and sighs. "I don't want to leave you."

"I don't want you to leave me either." I reply, maybe with a little hidden meaning in the backdrop. He leans in and plants a soft lush kiss on my mouth and begins to grow in intensity, opening my mouth to let him in he growls.

"If you keep this up, we will be doing it in your car."

I put my hands on his chest and he takes a small step back. "I'll talk to you later. Get home safe."

I sigh and open my car door. I roll down my window and watch his fine ass climb back onto his Ducati. Just the way his jeans tighten around his ass in the right way, makes me want to jump back on behind him. He throws his helmet on, winks at me, flicks the visor down and speeds off.

When I get home, I have about two hours before I am due at work. Oh I don't think so! So I decide to call in a favor owed to me by Dave. I have covered his shifts for the past two years now, and I have not once asked him to cover for me. It's time, Davey boy.

I pull out my cell when I get home.

"What do you mean, you're calling me in?" He sounds stunned.

"You know all those times you called me up at the wee hours of the morning begging me to cover your shift?" I rub it in deep.

He yawns. "You can't be serious."

"Oh, I am serious, boy! Get your butt up, because you're working this morning." I sound like a drill sergeant.

He groans unhappily. "This better be for a good reason. You never ask me to cover you. So what's up? Spill it, girl."

"I was out a little late last night and there is no way I am going to work a full shift today... Not while I have a hot date tonight..." I can't help but tell someone.

He gasps. "No! You have a *date* date? With whom, may I ask?"

"Oh, you don't know him, so don't worry about it. It's new so I don't want to share any details with anyone right now." I try to sound sincere, but it's hard when I want to yell from the rooftops, "I'M SEEING BEN MITCHELL!"

I can hear him rustling in the background and I am pretty sure I heard something break. He mumbles a "fucking shit" under his breath, which catches me off guard, because Dave doesn't typically swear. What's his deal? Oh, right probably rushing to get ready for his new shift, suck it up. "All right girl. Take care of yourself I hear he has a reputation... and you better tell me all the juicy details on our next shift together." He sounds borderline protective, curious and pissed off. *Whatever.*

"I will. Now get to work and I am off to bed." I announce and hang up.

I strip off my clothes and climb into bed. I fall asleep pretty fast. I wake up in in the late afternoon, to find a text from Ben:

Ben: *I hope the reason you're not answering your phone, is because you're asleep. And dreaming of me* ;)

There's that damn winky face again. He's playful. This is good.

Tess: *I was asleep and had very pleasant dreams, almost didn't want to wake up.*

Ben: *Well baby soon it won't be a dream.*

Tess: *So sure of yourself aren't ya?*

I have to tease him a little bit, keep him on his toes. Make him work for it a little bit, even though I can't resist him and I won't resist for much longer.

Ben: *Yes I am. Anyways, I will come pick you up for the show at seven.*

Tess: *Seven sounds great, gives me time to shower and get ready.*

I decide make him suffer a little.

Ben: *You're killing me. Slowly.*

Tess: *Isn't the anticipation, what makes it that much better?*

Ben: *I wouldn't know.*

Tess: *Oh that's right, you've always had women more than willing to sleep with you. No challenge.*

Ben: *I'm not going to lie, because that is true. The anticipation is only going to make the inevitable that much better.*

Oh, thank god he isn't here, because that anticipation would have been out the window by now!

Tess: *Alright Casanova, I am off to get ready, and make sure my camera's battery is charged and SD card is empty.*

Ben: *See you at seven Tess.*

I am all weak-kneed. Just from a few texts back and forth. Could I be any more juvenile?

I decide to throw hot pink streaks into my hair, put on plum eye shadow, and add black liner, mascara and a light pink glossy lip. For my outfit, I go with my black leather shorts and black tights underneath, a deep royal blue low neck tank top and a thin black scarf. For my shoes, I am bustin' out the big guns: my black patent leather Mary-Jane stiletto pumps.

At exactly seven, there's a knock on my door.

I creak open the door and give him a shy smile.

"You're killing me, Tess, look at you," he says. "You're stunning. I'll be fighting guys off of you all night."

I feel my face flush and my stomach turn as Ben holds a single red rose. "This is for you. It's not much, but a woman on the corner was selling them and I couldn't pass it up."

I smile and take the rose, and add it to the bouquet of peonies that he had given me.

"Shall we?" he asks, holding out his elbow to escort me out of the apartment. On the way through, I grab my bag and my little black faux leather coat with silver studs on the shoulders. Here goes everything.

Here goes my heart.

Chapter Fifteen

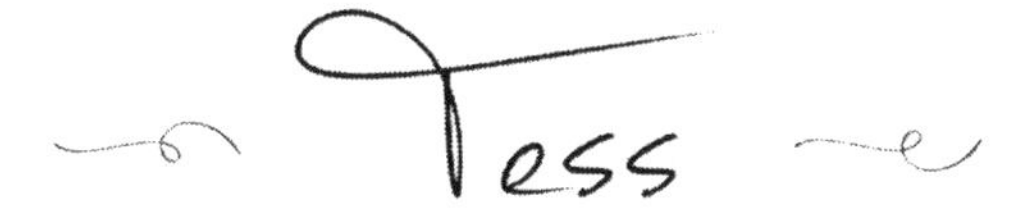

To my surprise, Ben has left his beloved bike at home and has picked me up in a car.

"Nice car," I tell him.

Obviously proud of his blacked-out vintage car, he begins, "It's a..."

I cut him off. "... nineteen-sixty-nine Pontiac GTO." I step away from Ben to take a walk around the machine and continue. "Top option, three hundred and seventy horsepower. Ram Air IV. Impressive."

Stunned, Ben takes a moment. "Uh, yeah. You...know cars?"

I make a slow walk back around the car to his side, trying not to fall in these heels. Right now, I am looking pretty badass in his eyes. "Yep."

"How?" He opens the passenger side door for me.

"James."

"Any other secret talents I should know about?"

"I'll let you know."

As we approach the backstage entrance at the arena, Ben places my dream "Press" laminate around my neck. It's funny how amazing you can feel while holding a piece of plastic tethered to a string, but for me it's a dream come true. "Ready?" he asks.

"More than you know." I reply, and in my head I add: *On more levels than one...*

People rush all around us. Some people are arguing, and others are running with sound equipment. I also see a lot of scantily clothed girls in here. Huh, so they are back here too? I am used to seeing them in the crowd flashing the bands, but I guess back here they have a better chance of scoring. One big-breasted brunette is actually wearing a bandanna as a top, and she approaches us.

"Beennnn," she drags out. "It's been too long, hunny, why haven't you called me?" She doesn't even acknowledge me on his arm. *Skank.*

"Uh, yeah...hi." Ben says, sounding a little shaken and grabbing for the back of his neck. I know he's been with other women—hell, a lot of other women—but I don't want to see it flaunted in my face. And this, this is what he went for? Wow, I feel a little more out of his league now.

Bandanna Skank traces her index finger down the center of his chest. "Come find me after the show." She smacks her lips, turns and leaves.

Ben looks down at me. "I am so sorry. I didn't think about running into any of my pasts here."

"It's fine, Ben. I know you've slept with other women." I am *not* that childish.

He leans down and kisses the top on my head. "Thank you for understanding. Most other women would have snapped and took off. I knew there was something different about you. You seem more mature than your actual age. By the way, how old are you? I never thought to ask."

"Twenty-two." I answer. "And yourself, Mr. Bond?"

"Mr. Bond? That's a new one. Twenty-five."

We approach a middle-aged man with headphones and mic holding a clipboard. Ben introduces himself, "Ben Mitchell, with *Tones* magazine. I am here to interview the band."

My jaw drops. Oh. My. God. I am going to meet Maroon 5? *Somebody pinch me, this can't be real.* And as if he can read my mind, Ben pinches my ass.

"Watch it, Bond." I snip, with a smile.

Mr. Clipboard breaks our stare. "Mr. Mitchell, the band will see you now. You have fifteen minutes." Ben nods and walks through the door, holding my hand.

The members of the band are sitting on leather sofas. A couple of them have a beer in their hands; they just look like they are relaxing before the big show. Their manager greets us as we walk in, and introduces us to the guys. Yeah, I feel like a schoolgirl...

Ben greets them with the traditional man hug, obviously having met and hung out before with them, and then he introduces me.

The lead singer approaches me. "Hey, I'm Adam." And he extends his hand. Trembling, I take it, and instead of shaking it, he kisses it.

"All right. Enough, dude," Ben says.

Adam laughs. "Sorry, I didn't mean to overstep a line. I was just being polite."

"It's OK. It's nice to meet you." I find my voice.

The guys look at one another and shake their heads, "Tess, it's OK, we get that a lot. But really we are just normal guys." Adam tries to make me feel more comfortable. But, really, have you seen the man? There is nothing normal about him.

"All right, wankers, I am here to do my job, so let me ask you a few questions, and we will be out of your hair. Then you can get out on stage," Ben says. "But first do you guys mind if Tess takes a few photos while we interview?"

"Oh, yeah, that's cool," Adam says.

Ben nods at me.

As Ben sets up a recorder and asks his questions, I move about the circle of guys and take as many shots as I can, from single band members to the whole group. And I do a few close-ups too. Wow, this feels amazing.

I can't help but take a few shots of Ben when he's not paying attention. This isn't easy, because he keeps looking at me whenever I move. I zoom in for a sharp side profile. *Man, I love some good jaw porn...* I snap one of his hands taking down notes. I capture this look in his eye of pure contentment and passion; he must really love this job. Who wouldn't? There is nothing sexier than a man with passion for life. He catches me staring and winks. Then nods toward the band, indicating that I should be taking their photos and not his.

"All right, thanks, guys, have a great show," Ben says, finishing up with the band.

I feel a little more relaxed now so I feel like I can actually speak up, "Thank you so much, guys. Oh! Would you mind signing my CD?"

"Yeah, of course." Adam answers, and the disc and a Sharpie are passed around the room.

We exit the room, walk through the crowded backstage area, and make our way to the side of the stage.

I continue taking photos of the opening bands, all while dancing with Ben. For all the fast songs we would mold our bodies together and move to the beat. For the slow ones he just held me, kissed me softly, and swayed. It was amazing. When Maroon 5 took the stage the crowd went absolutely nuts, I was able to stick my camera out just far enough to see the crowd, but not be seen. This is freaking awesome!

After the show, as the band came off of the stage, Ben grabbed one of the crew members and asked him to take a photo of us with the band. *I can now die a happy woman.* Ben wraps his arm around my waist on my right side while Adam takes the left and drapes his arm over my shoulder. Ben glares over at him and gives him a get your arm off of her or I will break it the fuck off look. Adam sneers and lets out a loud laugh, and pulls his arm away.

Adam speaks as he walks away. "Have your boyfriend e-mail me the pics. I wanna see." He stalks off into the crowd of girls and fans. Seriously? I look up at Ben and he nods, letting me know that he'll do it.

Ben takes my hand and leads me out to his beaut of a car. Before opening the door for me, like a perfect gentleman, he scoops me up into his arms, dips me and plants one hell of a hot kiss on me. The Seattle air is cold and crisp, but I don't even notice because I am on fire. When he releases me, I stumble back a little. Damn knees. He takes my hand and leads me into the car. "Your place or mine?"

"Yours." And with that we are off into the city, streamlining to his penthouse studio.

On the way back to Ben's place I am trying my damnedest to really figure out how I feel. How my body reacts to Ben, how my thoughts fill with dirty little visuals, but mostly how my heart swells when he looks at me and when he is so sweet and honest. He's protective and I need that in a man right now. But at the same time I am terrified that if I do sleep with him, and I just might tonight, that he will break my heart. Ben doesn't fuck a girl twice. Am I ready to let my walls fall down for him? And if I were to walk away, will I always wonder *what if?*

In the elevator, he rushes me to the back of the cart. Hands, mouths and tongues all over. Holy mother... I am ruined. I am going to sleep with Ben Mitchell tonight. It's a risk I am willing to take, because frankly I don't know if I will ever feel so passionately about another man.

The elevator doors open to his private hall. He has me walk ahead and he strides in behind me. He is right on my backside, curving with my body, kissing my neck. I can feel his erection at my back, turning me on more. I reach back and grab the growing bulge in his pants, and he moans. We somehow get inside and I turn and walk backwards into his kitchen, never taking my eyes off of him. He looks at me like I am prey and he is the predator ready to pounce. He starts to walk towards me, but I continue my backwards walk down the small hallway leading to his room. He grins that sexy smile.

I hold a hand up before my back hits the closed bedroom door.

"I need to ask you one question and you better fucking answer it honestly, and I'll know if you are lying."

He raises his right hand. "I swear."

"If I were to allow you to fuck me tonight, would you never do it again? Would you ask me to leave and never call you again?" I can hear the panic and sadness in my own voice. My hands start to tremble.

He places both hands gently on the sides of my cheeks and looks from my mouth to my eyes. "First. Tess, I don't plan to 'fuck' you tonight."

Oh. Well that's disappointing...

I look up to the ceiling, trying to fight back my tears. I knew he would change his mind. I am nothing like his past conquests. I am at least eight inches shorter, I have shorter hair and I wear glasses on most days. What would a man like Ben Mitchell want with a girl like me?

"Hey," he draws my attention back to his eyes, which are soft not mean like I was expecting. "Tess, like I said I am not going to 'fuck' you tonight, because I want to make love to you tonight." He says this in an almost whisper.

His mouth is on mine instantly, soft, gentle and loving. My heart isn't fighting any more right now, but absorbing every touch, smell and taste of this glorious man. I feel nervous of course, but not in the sense of it probably hurting a little, but that after tonight he will own me. Just like he said he wanted to.

We make our way into his room; he has the lights on a dimmer and keeps them lowered, comfortable. He sets me on the bed and kneels at my feet and unbuckles my heels. He slowly glides his hands up the outside of my legs. He unbuttons my shorts and pulls them and my stockings down in one slow agonizing motion. I am left sitting in my black lace thong, which I never wore before, and my royal blue top. I get up on my knees, while on the bed. We are chest to chest. I fist the hem of his shirt and bring it up to his shoulders, where he has to bend slightly, allowing me to finish the job. I throw it to the floor and now it's my turn to take his pants off. In his boxers, he grips my hips and rolls his hips into mine. I let out a low what sounds like a purr. *I had no idea I was capable of that...*

I step off of the bed to stand in front of him. His mouth is on my neck sucking and nibbling and then he whips my shirt right off. He steps back, a little too far for my taste, but stops three feet away. He looks from my feet to hips, belly and my black lace bra, and finally my eyes. And I can't take it anymore. I rush him. Full-on body slam. I stand on my tiptoes to meet his mouth. He doesn't resist me when I flick my tongue at his parting lips, but reciprocates with much-wanted force. He reaches around my back and undoes my bra, freeing my breasts. He lets it drop and he brings his mouth to one nipple and sucks. I grab the back of his head and walk backwards for the bed.

I lay back as softly and gracefully as I can, but poise is not my strong suit, and I fall over like a limp noodle. So not sexy. Ben lets out a soft quick laugh, and brings my knees up into a bend.

"I am going to assume you're not on the pill, seeing as you have had no reason to be." I don't know if he's asking or stating.

I blush and shake my head no.

"I don't normally keep condoms here, seeing as I have never had a girl here before, but I thought ahead in hopes this day would come and I stopped at the store before picking you up. Hold on." He hops off the bed and runs to the kitchen. Then the soft pads of his feet come thumping back into the room with a box in hand. He rips it open. Fast.

He resumes his position between my legs and brings his mouth to my belly. He kisses and sucks his way over every inch and nips at my left hip. I am so wound up that if he doesn't do something quick I am going to unravel before we get to the good stuff. He slips his hands under the waistband of my thong and instead of pulling them off, he rips them off. *Oh, all that is holy and fucking sexy.*

I slip my hand into the pocket of his shorts. Feeling how hard he is for me makes me want him that much more. To know that I do this to him is mind-blowing. He lets out a deep, low, animalistic growl and yanks down his boxers.

"Are you sure you're ready, Tess?"

"I have waited long enough. I am more than ready, but with you and only you." With my last words, he moans.

Kneeling before me, he strokes himself for a second before slipping on the condom. Oh screw me now, that is effing hot. He licks his lips in that little act of pleasure.

Lowering over me, he kisses me softly and I can feel him start to part my folds with his tip. Without thinking I instinctively raise my hips to meet his and his breath shakes when his tip slips into my moist flesh. Ooh. This is different.

"Slow, baby," he pleads. He slowly enters me. Filling me as slowly as possible, giving me a chance to adapt to his size. It pinches and stings for a short time, but it feels good. So good and so right. He never breaks eye contact with me. It's like he's trying to say something with his eyes, but I can't make it out. I start to become comfortable and I begin to move with him, in and out. Nice and slow. Raising and lowering my hips. I catch his eyes roll to the back of his head when I circle my hips, playing around with how it all feels.

"God, you're so tight," he groans. He begins to move a little faster. I can feel myself start to build. The depths of my belly and my core tremble and clench. I know I am close.

He growls. "Tess! Fuuu..." and with that I come. Hard, all around him. I feel my knees tighten around his hips.

I throw my head back. "Ben!" With that, he thrusts into me hard and his body ripples with his own release.

He stays inside of me for a few moments and we just stare at one another, me in amazement and awe, him I hope the same. He leans down and gives me the most gentle of kisses and slowly pulls out. I wince a little in discomfort.

"How was that?" I can't tell if he's being cocky or sincere.

All I can conjure up is a very, VERY satisfied sigh. He kisses my mouth and chuckles.

I wake up with the sun flooding the room with light. And the heat of Ben's long lean hot body coiled up into mine. Nine a.m. I have the perfect view of the fine tattoo work running from his chest and shoulder, down his arm. The black and gray work is crazy and the largest image looks like a stone angel, with the same black and gray work roses and smoke swirls. I can't help but trace the lines of his tattoos, and he stirs awake.

"Good morning, beautiful." His voice is sexy and sleepy.

Yum.

I give him a half smile. "Good morning yourself." I nudge my hips to his growing arousal.

Ben shrugs. "What? It's the morning and I have you in my bed. What would you expect?"

"An excuse to get me out the door, honestly," I admit.

"I told you. I am not letting you go."

I try to break the tension. "Well, how about letting me go, so I can get in a hot shower before you take me home?" I start to make my escape but feel his strong arms reach around my waist and pull me back down. All I can do is giggle.

"I like that sound," he says, nuzzling into my ear, sending shivers down my spine as I head for the shower. Ben, quickly at my heels, turns on the water and steam fills the all-white marble bathroom. We step in.

I still don't get it. I just don't know what he sees in me and I don't know if I ever will. I will just have to wait for him to get bored and to move on to the next girl that catches his eye. He will sleep with someone else while he's still with me. That's what men do, right? They say they are there for you and the next, they're gone. Or they don't get what they want, and with that thought, I shiver and my stomach churns. There is nothing I can do about Ben's past or his future endeavors, but I know I won't be his last.

"Hey." He breaks my depressing thoughts. "Where did you go?"

I just shrug and move my body into his. He squeezes silky body wash onto a loofa and starts to wash my back. Oh, this is heavenly. He massages my neck, and shoulders, and works his way down my back. And lower. He slips his fingers between my folds and rubs my mound, slowly, softly and he gradually begins to pick up pace. He slips one finger inside of me. I start to move my hips; this man makes me lose all control over my body. He can have it, it's his, and if he can do this to me in a few movements, my body is his for the taking.

I boldly reach back and grasp his rock-hard length *god I love how I have this effect on him...* A groan escapes him and his pace quickens, and so does mine. This is so animalistic, pleasing one another without even looking at each other. With his other hand, he reaches up to my breasts and rolls my nipple with his thumb and forefinger. I whimper under his touch, and he removed his fingers from inside me and presses down on my back, making me lose my grasp on him. He bends me over.

"Hands on the wall," he urges me, and I do what I am told. Holy hell, this is hot. "Hold on a second. Don't move," and he's out of the shower. He's back in a few moments, wearing a condom. I bite my lip in anticipation.

"This is going to be deeper this time," he tells me. Not knowing what to say or think, I nod. And then he thrusts hard and fast into me. Oh. My. God! I let out a scream, but not in pain but pure pleasure.

"Let it out, baby, I want to hear you. Don't hold back." He sounds demanding. So I let go, moaning and screaming with each thrust. His moans get deeper as he gets faster.

"Tess...fuck," he growls, and as he does, I let go. I scream his name and as my body convulses in his shower. The steam and the smell of him, the sound of him saying my name, just sends me through the roof.

After we start to come down, he turns me around and looks me in the eyes. He is breathing heavy and sporadically, just like me.

"I have never felt like this before. There is something you do to me, Tess. I can't get enough...obviously." He presses his forehead to mine and rests his eyes shut for a short moment.

I smile like a schoolgirl, and tip my head up and kiss him. He then steps out of the shower and grabs a large towel off the rack and wraps it around me as I step out.

"Thank you," I say with a smile. *And not just for the towel.*

While dressing, which by the way he had my clothes dry cleaned at some point since last night. I decide to ask him a question that's been on my mind.

"I was peeking at your amazing tattoo work this morning while you were sleeping," I begin.

"Which, by the way, I see that you have none," he says. This is true. I have wanted to get a tattoo since I was eighteen.

"I want one. I just want it to mean something."

"I think you'd look pretty hot with some ink."

"One day. So what's the meaning of yours?" I ask.

He is fetching a pair of his glorious fitted boxer briefs, when he stops and looks at his shoulder. I catch a soft warm smile crossing his face.

"It's for my mum," he answers.

I walk over to him and placc my hands gently on his chest, running my fingertips over the stone angel. "I think it is beautiful." I kiss his chest and I can feel him take in a deep breath of air.

"Thank you. She was an amazing woman."

"Come to dinner with me to my family's house tonight?" he asks me. Whoa, meeting the family? I don't think so.

"What?" I need to hear this again.

He drops his eyes to his shoes, puts his hands in his pockets and looks up through his lashes. "Come meet my family tonight."

I slowly shake my head. "Not yet." I say honestly. I don't want to hurt his feelings, even though he is opening up little by little, but I am not ready to do whatever it is we are doing in front of his family. I don't even know what we are yet.

"Why not?" he asks, slightly wounded.

"How would you even introduce me?"

"As mine," he says oh, so simply.

"Yours? Your what?" I'm getting a little irritated. "Look, don't worry about it, Ben. It's so soon yet for me to be introduced to your family. It doesn't feel right yet. I am sorry, but I am just not ready."

He sucks in a deep breath. "Are you seeing someone else? Is that why?"

Whoa! Where the hell did that come from? Now I am a little more than irritated. "First" I start. "I am not seeing anyone, nor have I seen anyone in the concept of dating or being someone's girlfriend, well, pretty much ever. Second, Ben, get over your shit! You have 'dated' so many women that I am sure I would want to puke if I heard the number. So let's not get all pissy with me, because you THINK I am seeing someone else." Boosh! Take that!

He grabs his keys and two helmets, opens the front door, and I grab my bag and rush past him. Not waiting for him at the elevator, I jump in and press the ground button. The doors begin to close, and Ben runs to catch it, but he's too late and I go down. His face was filled with worry and some anger, maybe even a little shock too...pfft. Probably never had a woman run away from him before.

I reach the lobby and practically run past the doorman, not allowing him to finish his "have a good day miss" spiel. Thank God it's a sunny day and not too cold. I manage about three blocks toward home in my heels when I hear the roar of a motorcycle zooming up the strip. The next thing I know, the tires of his Ducati screech to a halt just feet behind me next to the curb. He grabs my elbow and leads me into the Starbucks that we happen to be next to.

"What are you doing, Ben?" I could probably scream and have the cops here in the matter of minutes, but I think I need to get this off of my chest, because I know that if I don't now then I might never know. I won't cause a scene, but not because of him, but because

I don't feel like having any more sympathy from strangers. God knows I had plenty of that a couple of years ago...

"What do you want, Ben?" I continue. "Typically you fuck girls and tell them to get lost and then we do it and I leave before you can tell me to get the hell out and you panic?"

"I know, I know." He slumps into an empty chair and I sit next to him.

He turns his body and continues, "I am just as confused as you are, if not more. It wasn't right of me to accuse you of seeing someone else, I am sorry for that. But I have my reasons."

Oh really? "I'm listening." I urge him on with the roll of my hand.

"I was engaged once."

Oh.

He sucks in a deep breath of air. "We dated in high school. We went to the same college freshman year. We didn't want to separate, so we decided to apply at all the same schools. I proposed to her at the end of our junior year. We were engaged to be married."

Not what I was expecting to hear. "And...?"

He scrunches his face. "And...I caught her with our Western Civ professor. I was going to his office to talk about an upcoming exam. When I knocked there was no answer, the door was unlocked so I went in. I caught them right on his desk."

"Oh, I am so sorry...well, kind of." If he's looking for honesty, well, here it is.

He laughs lightly, but it doesn't reach his eyes. "Yeah, I know. Better I had found out before the wedding, right?" he asks.

"Honestly, Ben," I say, and pause for a second trying to scan through what I am about to say for something wrong, but I have no filter right now. "I am glad it didn't work out with her, because I never would have had a chance with you. But I am not her. I am nothing like her. So don't ever EVER accuse me of being something or someone I'm not."

"I know." He grabs my hand and invites me to sit on his lap. I ease into the rich green velvety chair he's occupying, ignoring any stares we may be getting. I don't care.

"So, is that why you never dated or held a serious relationship? You were afraid of getting hurt again, weren't you?" I ask as softly as I can.

He nuzzles my neck and I can feel him breathe in my hair. Taking my breath away from me, making me feel something I have never felt before and it's not just the lust I feel for him, but something more.

"I think so. I think that's why I haven't ever attached myself to anyone before. Do you know what it's like to lose all faith in one group of people? I think I lost my trust in all women, until I met you. That scares the shit out of me, Tess. I don't want to be hurt that way again. I gave my whole being to Nicole and she tossed it aside like a scratched CD."

And I do know exactly what he means and how he feels. I had no faith or trust in any straight man other than my brother.

I nod and caress the sides of his face with my hands, and look him in the eyes. "I do."

Hearing her name rings a bell immediately. I remember the bimbo at Chatz. He never did explain who she was...he distracted me with his sexiness. "That was Nicole at Chatz last night, wasn't it?" I ask him.

He looks at me and nods slowly. "I guess I never did get to that point of the story that night, did I?"

I purse my lips. "No, you didn't. Instead you distracted me with your...well, you know."

"Yeah, sorry about that. It wasn't my intention to distract you from the situation. It's just that you make me forget all about that pain. You make life that much more bearable. You make it amazing."

I don't say anything for a moment. He softly rubs the small of my back. "Think we should order something before they kick us out for inappropriate touching?" He winks.

"Sure, I haven't come nearly close to my daily quota of caffeine intake." I giggle as he tickles my side. He takes my hand and leads me to the counter.

Leaning in, he asks, "What'll it be, Punky?"

I scrunch my face. "Punky?"

He gives me an ear-to-ear grin. "You heard me." I roll my eyes at the nickname. Damn Erin.

I speak in a low, sultry voice. "I'll take a tall, dark with a triple shot with caramel and whip cream on top." I end with a lick of my lips.

He closes his eyes. "Keep it up," he growls in my ear, "and I'll have you in a Starbucks restroom."

Oh my.

He then places his order: "I'll just have a venti black coffee."

He looks back at me. "I'm simple, unlike someone I know who has to list off twenty things just for a cup of coffee." He winks and bumps my shoulder.

"What can I say? I like what I like, and I am not afraid to get it." I tell him, and I know he knows what I mean.

We get our drinks and sit. "So tell me about your sister," I say. "You spoke very highly of her the other day."

His loving smile crosses his mouth. I like seeing him at ease and happy. "She goes to a private school here in the city, straight A's, and a little fashionista in training. She designs all of her clothes, never buys anything off the shelves. She has this sense of drive just like me and my father; that's how my mum was too. I like to look out for her and protect her. She calls me every other day to keep me in the loop. Now how many little sisters do you know that would confide so much in their big brother?"

"I do know what that's like. I am close to James.

I hope I meet Caroline one day."

He grunts and shifts his weight. "I invited you over today and you declined." Oh, right. Crap.

"Ben, I am sorry. It's just like you said about learning to trust someone. This is all new to me as well. I need to figure it all out." I feel like total shit now.

"What do you need to figure out? I am crazy about you. I am trying here. I am gaining faith and trust in you, in us."

I sigh. “I know. Please trust me?”

“OK.” I know he means it just from the tone in his voice and the look in his eyes. This man cares for me, just as I do for him. We are both slightly broken and with enough faith we can mend our wounds together...once I can work up the courage to discuss my battle wounds.

He walks me up to my door and kisses me on the forehead. “I am going to call you tomorrow. No hiding.”

He rushes me with a full-blown, knee-melting, mind-twirling, heat wave kiss. Then pulls away and smacks my butt playfully. “Bye, Punky” he says. Winks, and he’s off.

I swoon.

Chapter Sixteen

When I get in, I notice that I didn't even unlock my door. *What the hell?* I remember locking it up, didn't I? Nothing is messed up. I take a look around. All of my electronics are here, TV, stereo, CD's and DVD's. Maybe I just forgot to lock up.

I text Erin, I need girl time. Wanna hang?"

"Hell's yeah! Let's go shopping!" Erin replies. Oh, it's been a while since I have gotten a new outfit.

She'll pick me up in twenty minutes. I change into some jeans, a gray thermal shirt with a cute royal blue scarf, and my black over-the-knee boots.

We decide to hit up the mall since it's raining now. Damn Seattle weather and its mood swings. At least at the mall, it's dry and warm.

"So, are you going to tell me what's going on?" Erin says.

I go into all the details about going backstage, meeting the band, taking some photos, and then going back to his place.

"Did you?" she blurts out, causing a few passers-by to glance in our direction.

"Did I what?" I play innocent.

"Oh, you know what I mean, girl! Spill it! Like right now!"

I smile from ear to ear. "Yep," is all I say, and she screams loud enough to make the nearby people go deaf.

"How was it?" She bounces with excitement.

I sigh. "Really, *really* good."

All she says is "nice" and I willingly give her the juicy bits she was looking for, but she didn't have to ask. I trust Erin, which is a major thing for me.

We continue to talk about my sexcapades while skimming the racks for good deals. "When are you seeing him again?" she asks.

"I don't know. He invited me to his family's house for dinner tonight, but I told him no. I'm not ready for that yet."

She nods like she understands, and she probably does. "Well, in that case let's get you a smokin' dress, so when you do know you're going to see him again you'll knock him dead."

Chapter Seventeen

I pulled another double at the café today, before my evening art class. I'm kind of bummed that we are done with the human form lesson. Seeing as I won't be able to stare at Ben for an hour and a half...then again I don't want anyone else looking at him naked ever again.

Dave called in with the flu, so it's probably a good thing that I came early, that I beat him to the punch of asking me for the favor. The day goes by pretty quickly, even though I am constantly looking at my phone every chance I get to see if Ben tried calling or texted me. Nothing. *Don't be that girl, Tess, don't be the girl who waits desperately for the guy to call, he said he'd call though...damn it! Knock it off! He'll call.*

About an hour before my shift ends, with six cups of coffee in my system, he calls...finally.

"Hey baby, what are you doing?" He's casual.

I give him the bare facts.

He drops his voice. "Dave?"

"Gay."

His voice goes up a notch. "Good." *Yeah, no worries, Benny boy, that boy very much so enjoys the cock, so I have heard...over and over.*

"What about you? Aren't you supposed to be working?" I tease.

"I am. Just adding the final touches to the Maroon show piece." Ah, I love thinking about that night, and soon I will get to see it in my favorite magazine. And by my favorite columnist, who just so happens to be my...well, not sure what to call us yet.

"What are you doing after work?"

I tell him, and he lets out a soft laugh. "Too bad, I'm not going to be there, huh? How will you ever get through it?"

"I don't know, Ben."

A moan invades my ear. "I love it when you say my name." He says as his accent rolls and deepens, when he is aroused, which in turn turns me on.

"Ben."

"Tess, stop or I'll come in and drag you to the back room."

"Hey, I've got to get back to work before my boss fires me for being late coming back from break. Rather than be fired for screwing in the stockroom." I snort.

He full-on laughs. "I suppose so. OK, have a good class. Bye."

I am five minutes late, rushing, remembering the chat Ms. S. and I had last week. I nearly face-plant as I trip over an extension cord. *Son of a bitch...* I can't sneak in unseen, can I? I avoid any eye contact with the other students and with Ms. S., who is laying out what looks like yards upon yards of rolled white fabric. I notice a few fans set up around the room, what the hell do we need fans for? It's almost freezing outside tonight, so it definitely doesn't need to be cooled down in here. Everyone has a strip of the fabric, little tubes of ink, rubber blocks and X-acto knives.

I scavenge for supplies as Ms. S announces that we are doing block inking tonight, and she wants us to etch a few designs in the rubber blocks and roll different-colored inks onto its surface, then transfer it to the fabric. But the images have to be related and create a story.

I decide for my first to carve London's Big Ben. Yeah, my theme is Ben. Yeah, Ben on the brain tonight, but that's OK though because I don't think anyone here is going to get it. For my second, I etch a phone. For the private message he sent me, that first night. The first private message he had ever sent. I smile at that thought. I used a metallic silver ink for this one and I press the rubber to the crisp white fabric. Now, for my third, I try to think of a way to visually sum up what we are now. I can't scratch the word *sex* into the block, for god's sake!

Ms. S. sees me in deep thought, tapping my knife on the rubber.

"Carver's block?" she jokes.

I chuckle. "Yeah, I guess you could say that. I just can't think of the last design I want to use to tell my story."

"Well, tell me about the first two. That is, if you are comfortable in doing so."

I take in a quick breath. "This new guy I am seeing is from London, hence the Big Ben, but that's his name also, Ben." As I am explaining I am deepening some of the lines in the peak of the Big Ben when Ms. S. squeals.

"Ben? As in the Ben who was last week's model Ben?" She is full of excitement and shock. Why?

"Uh, yeah."

"Ben is my boyfriend's son. Oh, God, Tess!" She screams the last part so fast and loud that I jumped with the news and slipped with my knife.

"SHIT!" I scream. Holy hell, I am bleeding really badly! I sliced right between my left thumb and index finger. I hear some students panic; one passes out from the sight of my growing pool of blood. And one rushes over with a wad of the white fabric she was using for her project. I wrap it around my wound and the fabric fills with a spreading red stain.

"Tess, I have to take you to the emergency room!" Ms. S. says as she pulls me to my feet. "Uh, class dismissed." We rush out the door.

Ms. S. is the most terrifying driver I have ever witnessed. Speeding like a bat out of hell, speeding through a few red lights and slowing for the yellows. Yeah, I know that makes no freaking sense to me, either. At the ER, she pulls up to the doors and a waiting man opens my door and helps me out. Noticing the fabric filled with blood—a lot of it now running down my arm—he leans his head to a speaker on his shoulder, presses a button, and tells them "alert triage," because apparently I'm a "bleeder."

Mrs. S was alert enough to grab my bag, with my ID and insurance card.

A few seconds later a nurse takes me to triage. I start to feel faint as the blood keeps seeping down my arm. It's now soaking my pants. The nurse asks me questions but as soon as I tell her my name I black out.

I wake up in a hospital bed. Tubes with red liquid lead to my right hand, where an IV needle is embedded. Then I remember why I am here, and lift my left hand to see a huge bandage. Great. *Just great, you really did it this time, Tess.* I rest my head back just as a handsome middle-aged doctor enters the room.

"Tess Martin? Hello, I am Doctor Mitchell. How are we feeling?" He speaks in a familiar English accent.

I try to speak but my mouth is so dry. He reaches for a foam cup filled with ice water and hands it to me. I take a small sip from the straw, and it is heavenly in my hot dry mouth.

"Mmm...better now." I reply. *Oh, yep I feel some morphine.*

Hello.

He lets out a light chuckle like Ben does...ah, Ben. "Well, that's good. You had a nasty slice, took all of seventeen stitches, but I don't predict any nerve damage. You were pretty lucky, young lady."

"Well, that's good, and thank you." Pretty sure I slurred that a little.

"Once they paged me, telling me that Gwen had brought in one of her students, I ran right down to attend to you. She speaks very highly of your work."

"Gwen?" I ask.

"Ms. Sawyer," he clarifies.

I nod my head and it feels like it's going to roll right off my body.

"You know what, Tess, you look vaguely familiar. Have I treated you before?" he asks, a little weary. I don't think he's ever treated me...

He squints slightly, then speaks before me. "Were you in here a few years back after a concert incident?" he asks me. *Uh...oh my god.*

I can feel tears filling my eyes and I am sobering up from the morphine. "Yes," I manage.

"Oh, sweetheart. I am sorry I didn't mean to upset you. It's just that you looked really familiar, maybe it's because it was my son who brought you in that night and asked me to treat you." He explains and I think I am going to be sick.

Ben. Ben was the one who saved me from my attacker? Ben was the one who drove me to the hospital? Ben was the one who just dropped me off and left me alone? Alone, after nearly being raped and then trampled on by God knows how many people?

I think I am going to be sick. The room is starting to spin and the doctor is rushing to my side. I see a blur of blue scrubs surrounding both sides of the bed. I feel the blood pressure cuff squeeze my arm and I hear the beeping of the monitors. My mind is swirling, not just for being forced to remember that night at the concert, but waking up in the hospital all alone, not knowing how I got there. And now I find out its Ben who had delivered me. It was Ben's father who treated my broken arm and fractured nose and dressed a few gashes.

I hear the doctor calling my name, trying to get me to focus and speak. "Tess. Tess, can you hear me?" he keeps repeating.

"Yeah," I let out after a moment.

Checking all of my vitals he continues to ask questions. "I didn't mean to bring up any unpleasant memories, Miss Martin. It's just my son went to great lengths that night to ensure that you became my patient."

"Ben? Ben Mitchell is your son?"

"Yes, dear, he is." He is checking my IV. "I assumed you knew Ben since that night."

"No, we just technically met as of recently."

I see a confused look on his handsome, distinguished face.

I can feel my cheeks fill with the new blood that has been transfusing through my body. "We are sort of seeing one another." I admit. And in a way, I'm admitting it to myself.

He smiles from ear to ear. "Ben spoke of a girl last night at dinner, but he didn't mention it was the beautiful girl who I bandaged up those few years ago."

"I don't think he knows it was me, sir," I say in a respectful tone.

"Please, darling, you're seeing my son, call me Jack." His tone is friendly and loving.

I just nod. I am not sure how I am feeling right now, and I don't mean my body, or the hand I so viciously sliced open.

"How long have I been here?" I ask.

Jack Mitchell takes a look at his gold watch and then at the clipboard in his hand. "Looks like Gwen dropped you off about three hours ago. Do you want me to call anyone?"

Do I? Do I want him to call my mom? No, she would just spaz out. Do I want him to call Erin? No, I can't explain any of this right now. It's bad enough that Ben's father knows even more than Ben does about that night. God, this is so messed up. James would ask too many questions.

Before I can answer, he says, "Want me to call Ben?"

My heart is pounding. I don't know if I can confront this tonight. Then again, I may as well get it over with...

"Sure." I answer.

I can feel my eyes start to get moist as I listen to Jack fill in his son on what happened. My feelings are mixed.

"OK, I will let her know. Bye son." He hangs up with Ben, then looks at me. "He's on his way."

And I breathe.

Chapter Eighteen

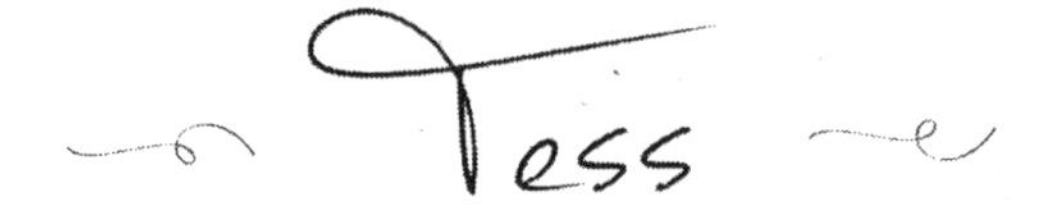

They've cut off my morphine. I want to rage at the nurse until she brings me something for the pain in my hand.

I wonder if Jack will explain that I am the one he brought in that night. I hope not. I want to tell him. Then there's a knock on my door. My chest starts to pound. Ben peeks in and in a few long strides, he's next to me. He leans in and kisses me hard on the mouth. Oh, now that's a way to forget about the pain.

Holding my face, he looks me all over, and then coils back to look at my heavily bandaged hand. "How are you feeling? When my dad called to tell me you were here I thought the worst, I thought I was about to snap and lose it all."

"I am fine. I just cut my hand pretty bad and lost a lot of blood, but I have been refueled, so no worries." I try to pull this off like it's nothing.

"God, I am so relieved that you are OK." He sounds breathless. I don't want him to feel relief, because I don't feel relieved. I want him to feel the hurt that I have felt for the past three years!

I have to do this. "It was you."

"What was me?"

My eyes start to sting from trying to hold in my tears. "It was you who brought me to this same hospital three years ago."

He just looks at me.

"At the concert, Ben! I was just about to be raped and you attacked the guy, but by the time you got back to me, I was trampled to a fucking bloody pulp! Then you bring me here to be seen by your father, and then you leave! You just left me." I can't help the screaming and the now-heavy crying. This is something that I have held back every day since that horrible night. Not letting anyone know about what happened.

His eyes are wide. He stands and steps away, but doesn't leave the room. "That was you?"

"Yes, that was me. You would have known that if you didn't abandon me at a hospital like you just found a motherless infant by a dumpster! That's how I feel, I feel like I was so unwanted, not worth the time to wait and see if that girl was going to be OK. But you couldn't do that, could you, Ben?"

He drops his head into his hands. I can see the defeat overcoming him; he doesn't know what to say to me, and I don't think there is anything he could say to make me not hate him. So I go on, getting it all out, just like how I have wanted since that night to the guy who tried to force himself onto me, and to the guy who started out the hero and in the end became the villain.

"Before that show I was already tortured and tormented every day. My father didn't give a shit about me or the way I wanted to live my life. My only friend was my mother. I never had a real boyfriend, because I was the weird girl. Music was my escape, that's why I love it so much. I am free to be who I am and love what I love.

"That's why I was at that show that night, as you know James normally went with me, but he couldn't go that night so I went alone. I wasn't going to miss this show. I was having a pretty bad week, so this was my night to vent. Everything was fine until the headliners were halfway through their set, when this guy started rubbing himself up on me from behind. Not wanting that kind of attention, I told him to get lost and to look elsewhere. He didn't take no for an answer. Not the first time, the second, third fourth or fifth. I turned to slap him and he punched me in my stomach and I dropped. I tried to stand but he backhanded me across my face.

"I couldn't talk, I couldn't think. The next thing I know I am on my back on the sticky beer-soaked floor and this guy is over the top of me, grabbing my chest, licking my neck, and then he started to undo my pants, then his own. Then he was gone.

"But I was so dazed and lost, and before I could get up people started a mosh pit next to me. I was stomped on, kicked into. I have flashes of being in a car and seeing the city lights passing above my head. Then on a gurney being wheeled down a bright hallway. Then it's morning and I am all alone in a hospital room, alone. I didn't know where I was and how I got there.

"Then I realize my worst fear, was I raped the night before? Did that horrible human being take something so personal and private away from me? After an exam they revealed that I wasn't, but that didn't make me feel any better. I just can't wrap my head around a guy who saves a girl, and then abandons her."

That's my story. He has to make his choice now. Stay or go. The same decision he faced three years ago.

Chapter Nineteen

~ Ben ~

I am so stoked. This is my big chance to prove myself at the magazine. They finally gave me the opportunity to cover a show by myself. Before, I was an assistant and a go-fer. It's not the sold-out kind of show I want to cover, but hey, I got to start somewhere, right?

While one of the opening bands is on stage, I get to conduct my interview with the lead band. I know their stuff, and they fucking rock! *Keep it cool dude, keep it cool.* I finish, pack up, make my way to the side stage to watch the show. This is my dream job. I get to hang around some of the people I love and idolize, and be up close and personal to the stage.

I high-fived the last opening band as its members passed, clearly on a total adrenalin high. The closest I ever got to that feeling was doing a few small-ass shows with Dan in our senior year of high school. We weren't exactly the most kick-ass band in town, but we had fun. And I learned how to play bass pretty good. Man, those were good times. But when he went to college on the east coast and I stayed here on the west, to go to school with Nicole we didn't see each other much, therefore no play time. And with my best friend and band mate gone, I stopped playing.

The front-liner band, the one I just go to know and interview, run past me to take the stage. I know this is going to be good. They are just starting their fourth song in the set, something fast and upbeat, and the crowd is getting amped. I can already see a few smaller mosh pits being formed. I see girls flashing the band. Holy shit! Yeah, I will definitely be trying to hook up with one of those girls tonight. I need to get laid!

I see a short blonde girl dancing with some douchebag a few rows back. She doesn't look too happy; the guy behind her is grinding her ass pretty good. She looks really upset. What, trouble in paradise, babe? I can't help but watch this lover's quarrel. But something doesn't feel right, and I don't normally feel anything towards a girl or her feelings. Not since I caught Nicole fucking our professor. But this girl in the crowd, there's something going on. Something I don't like.

I see the guy punch her in the stomach. What the FUCK? What the fuck is that asshole doing? She can't be any taller than five foot three, and doesn't look more than hundred pounds. She's gone. Where is she?

Shit.

I run to the side exit door, to get into the crowd, I shove past the security guards and make my way to where I saw her standing. I finally spot her and she's on the floor trying to stand up, but then the motherfucker backhands her right across the face. Why am I even caring? What if this is their normal relationship? Foreplay, perhaps? No.

I push and shove my way through the crowd to reach the douchebag. I can't hold back; it's like I lost all control of my body. Just like how I was before we left London. I grab his shoulder to pull him off her and I see that his pants are undone, and I notice that her pants are just below her hips. Was this fucker going to rape her? And as if in a movie, the perfect song starts to play from the band on stage, one that plays what's going on in my head. The lead singer growls out, "When my fist hits your face, and your face hits the floor. It'll be a long time coming. Bet you got the message now. 'Cause I was never going. Yeah, you're the one that's going down."

I have him on the ground in the back of the room, straddling him, and my fist meets his face, blasting away, and I don't stop until one of the security guards pushes me off of the guy. I look down at him. He isn't moving. I can't even make out any facial structure.

"Hey, man you gotta get out of here, before someone calls the cops," the security guy says to me, but I can barely hear a thing he's saying between the music and the blood coursing through my ears. I remember the girl.

Running back to where she was, I don't see her. I keep going in that direction when I see her still on the floor. Not moving. Shit. There are mosh pits in full force on both sides of her. I see a few larger guys in boots kicking into her, not even seeing her lifeless body on the ground. I bend down and scoop her up. *Damn, she is a tiny little thing…too bad I can't see her sweet face, it's covered in so much blood…*

People barely move as they see me carrying her out of the building. Jerks. As I walk to my car (thank god I chose that tonight over my bike), I keep checking to make sure she is breathing. Man, her nose is messed up, and she has a lot of cuts on her face. One particularly long one on her cheek from when she got slapped. I swear to God if I didn't kill that fucker tonight, he will be done if I ever see him again.

I open the back door of my vintage black GTO and lay her gently across the back seat. Christ, any other day, if I have a girl in my car, if she even looks like she might puke I won't let her in. This car is my baby, right along with my bike, and typically I won't have anything in it that could stain or rip the interior, but I don't seem to care that her blood will stain the shit out of my backseats. I just need to get her to the hospital, and I hope my dad is working tonight.

I pull up to the emergency room entrance and the attending physician looks in the back seat. I can tell by his face that he assumes I did something to her. That I hurt her. The thought sickens me to my core. He opens the door and sees all of the blood and her disjointed body and calls for backup. I start to get out of the car to help when the guy tells me, "You can't park it here. You can go park your car in the visitor lot over there." He nods in the direction of the lot.

I jump back in, close my door and I watch them load her on to a gurney and wheel her in through the sliding doors. Shit, what am I going to do? I walk back into the hospital, hoping that they got her back right away. I walk to the admitting desk and approach the young pretty attendant.

"Excuse me, hi, that girl that was just brought through can you make sure that Jack Mitchell attends to her? That's my father and I want him to treat her." I sternly tell the girl, who is obviously mind-stripping me. Yeah, I get that all the time, sweetheart.

She puckers her lips and bats her eyes. "Of course, I'll page him right away. Would you like to speak to him yourself, Mr. Mitchell?"

"Yes, please." I take a seat.

I feel a hand on my shoulder about fifteen minutes later. "Ben? What's going on? I was told to see the young woman who was just brought in. I just looked her over and she is pretty banged up. What happened?"

I hear a little accusation in his voice. What did I expect? I was thrown out of three schools in four years back in London for tearing people up. But I would never lay a finger on a woman, especially one as small as her.

I explain, and I hope from what I described, he can treat her better.

He nods, and I think he believes me, "I will have the attending OB/GYN examine her, if that's the case. And the rest, well, I can fix her up."

I nod.

"Do you want to wait to see her?" my father asks. Do I? I shouldn't care.

I think about it for a moment. "No. I don't even know the girl. What good would it do if I stayed? I would probably just freak her out. Finding some weird guy waiting around for her."

He nods. "I'll see you at Sunday's dinner then?"

"Yep." And then my father is off, back to work.

I don't know how to take care of someone other than Caroline, but that's different. Maybe I can ask Dad about how she is in a few days. Maybe I should just forget about it. I have no fucking idea. I am sitting in a hospital waiting room wracking my brain on what I should do, seeing that helpless girl on the floor so hurt...I don't know.

I'm not ready to handle something like this. I got to get out of here. I need a drink and a pair of legs to get lost between, hopefully that'll take the edge off.

What's wrong with me?

Chapter Twenty

Tess

I feel much better this morning when I wake up in the hospital bed. Well, physically better. My heart could use some work.

Apparently I can't just call a taxi to come get me, and I am forced to decide between calling my mom or Erin. I could call James, but he already feels the need to protect me, and I don't want to worry him anymore. Ugh, if I don't call my mom and ask her to get me, she will eventually find out and rip me a new one.

"Tess! Where have you been? I have been trying to get a hold of you the past few days." Yup, that's my mom, not even a hello, just straight to the point. Gotta love her.

"I have been really busy at work, school and I even made a new friend."

"Oh, that's great, Tess! We will have to get together this week and catch up." Ha. Little does she know that time is now.

I sigh. "That's why I am calling, Mom. I kind of need you to pick me up at the hospital."

She gasps. "Oh my God, sweetie! What happened? Why didn't you call me sooner? What hospital? I am on my way. What happened?"

I tell her which hospital and what floor. "I'll explain everything when you get here OK, mom?"

She promises she'll be there in twenty minutes.

As I wait, I glance at my phone and see that Ben never tried to call or text me. After I spilled my heart and guts all over the floor for him about that night, he didn't say anything. Couldn't give me one good answer to as why he didn't stay to see if I was all right. Not one damn word. He just walked out the door...again.

Whatever. I knew it would happen. He got what he wanted and this was his perfect opportunity to get out. Picking an angst song on my iPod, I close my eyes and just breathe.

I must have fallen asleep, because when I open my eyes my mom is next to my bed just staring at me. *Yeah like that's not going to make my blood pressure spike!*

"Jesus! Mom!" I scream. "What is wrong with you? You almost gave me a heart attack!"

She looks sad. "I am sorry, Tess. I was just thinking about when you were a little girl and you were having a pillow fight with your friends and you slipped on one, and fell face first into the wooden coffee table. Cracking your head right open and needing stitches."

I touch my forehead where the scar is still visible, even now. "Mom, I am sorry I didn't call you last night, I was just so tired from the stitches, blood transfusion, and being doped up on morphine."

"Blood transfusion? What the hell happened, Tess?" Oh, here we go, ladies and gentlemen, Miss. Blowing Things Out of Proportion is up to plate! *OK, maybe I get a little of that from her myself...*

I sigh, take in a deep breath of air, and tell the story. I blame her for my clumsy gene. I leave out all of the Ben parts, though. It's not worth it to him, apparently, so I may as well forget all about it myself.

As I check out, I am told to set up an appointment with Dr. Mitchell in a week. Shit! So much for forgetting about Ben, huh?

I gather up my bag and put one arm through my jacket, seeing as I have a massive bandage/cast thing compassing most of my left hand. At the outpatient entrance, the nurse who was attending me last night approaches me.

"So, that guy that came to visit you last night, he was really hot. Like really hot." She's gushing in a not so professional manner but I indulge her.

"What about him?"

She smiles mischievously and hands me a small piece of paper. "Can you give him my number?" *What the...*

"What the fuck? Are you kidding me? Are you trying to hook up with a guy that you don't even know and for all you do know, but don't seem care, that he just might be MY boyfriend?"

She eyes me, in my wheelchair. "Honestly, I think I am more his type." She turns and leaves.

Seriously? I look down at the paper with the number scribbled on there—in pink ink, nonetheless—gag—and consider shredding it up. But you know what, if I ever do see Ben again, why should I cock-block him? I'll give it to him *yeah shove it right up his ass...*

At home, I call James. I know he would have visited me in the hospital, but he has a life and is busy with his new job, designing this new building in the city.

I tell him what happened.

"You should have called me, Tess," he says, "no matter what I was doing at the time, it's not as important as you will ever be. I mean it." He gushes, aww my big brother the softy, but I love him for that.

"Either way I am fine, I am home safe and sound."

He sighs with obvious relief and promises to see me tomorrow.

"I love you," he says, "have a good night and tell your mom I said hi."

I get out of the shower; my mom is still out getting food. I reach for my iPod when my phone buzzes.

"1 private message"

Shit. Chatz chat room. How the hell did I never log out? Still woozy from the meds, I open it without thinking.

Big_Ben: *I'm sorry.*

This time I log out. Turn my phone off. I want a drink, but I know I can't because of the freaking meds. I'm feeling a little pissy now. I stomp to my music dock instead and crank up some Shinedown and start belting out my voice along with the lyrics about being worn out and that it's over. *Is it over?*

Now if I could only open a tube of paint and really let loose...damn hand. My door opens and my mom walks in with food. "What are you doing? You're supposed to me resting and I find you in here moshing?"

"The music is calming me down."

"That loud? How can that be relaxing?"

I smile and shrug.

My mom knows me well enough to not get on me about listening to music. I return my butt to the couch *the same red couch that Ben had kissed me on. The same couch I felt something for him on.* As I eat, we chitchat about Mom's job at the bank and my schoolwork. Once we are finished eating, I can barely keep my eyes open, so my mom helps me to my bed and tucks me in. Yes, actually tucks me in. And you know what? It's really nice.

She kisses my forehead. "Get some sleep, sweetie. I'll call you tomorrow."

"I love you too, Mom, and thank you for everything."

I am awakened by a pounding on my front door. that or my pain meds wore off and I am dying.

"Tess Martin, I know you're in there, and you are a horrible best friend for not calling to inform YOUR best friend that you were hospitalized!" It's Erin.

I groan, roll my eyes, and slowly make my way to the front of my apartment. "I'm coming." I grumble.

"Hey you," I greet her as soon as she's inside, as innocent-sounding as possible.

"Don't you 'hey' me, Missy! Once I heard that some art geek was rushed to the ER for an accident, I knew it was you. Why didn't you tell me? Call or text me?"

Wait. "Art geek?"

She throws her hands up in the air. "Yeah, I overheard some of my business classmates talking, when I heard...their words not mine."

I tell her the story but leave out the Ben drama.

"Holy crap, girl! I am so sorry for even being upset. I was just so worried. I know we haven't been friends that long, but I think of you like a sister." Her admission warms my heart; I have always wanted a sister.

I sigh and lean in for a one-handed hug and kiss her on the cheek. "Thank you for worrying, and I love you too, Erin, you and your dirty mind." I finish with a wink. Then she brings up what I was really hoping she wouldn't bring up...

"So, did Ben come to see you in the hospital last night?" From her tone I can't tell if she knows something or not.

"Um...yeah."

She cocks her head to one side. "And? You sound leery on the topic. What happened?"

"Well, I don't think we will be seeing each other any longer." And as easy as it came out, it's not so easy to accept. I started to trust Ben; it was all feeling good. But knowing what I know now ...

She eyes me suspiciously. I have never had a great poker face. "There's something you're not telling me. I want to know what's got you so hush-hush. You may as well just tell me, before I torture it out of you."

"Can you accept the quick version?" She nods.

I tell her the story of the concert. The one three years ago.

"Ben was the one who saved me," I conclude. And with that statement, my head cleared. I no longer felt the static of an off-air TV channel, but rather the picture is coming in clear, digitally clear. *Ben saved me.*

I gasp and throw my hands to my face, and start to sob. I let it all out. I laid some heavy stuff on him last night and he left. He didn't even feel the need to tell me his side of the story. I shouldn't have blown up at him the way I did, but I have never talked to anyone about what had happened that night. But what hurts the most is he didn't feel strong enough to talk about it, then or now. He chose to walk away a second time.

Erin, being the amazing friend she is, can read me like a book. "You should call him, Tess." She didn't say it like her normal, 'call him for some booty' kind of call. She looked soft around her edges, which was a different side to Erin. I was used to the ball-buster Erin.

As much as I would love to hear his voice right now, I just don't think I could bring myself to do it. I told him everything and he chose to, well, he didn't choose me. I'm just not worth it.

"No. I don't think that's a good idea, Erin."

And she leaves it at that.

"So how are things with Mark?" I change the topic.

"Well, he's at work a lot. I seem to only get the booty call at two a.m." She says with an eye roll.

It doesn't take a dummy to see that even though she is playing it off as nothing, it hurts. "I know you're a nympho and all, but I know you better than that Erin."

"Know what?"

I give her forehead a little smack with the palm of my hand, "That you really have feelings for the guy. You just need to tell him. Life's too short. And from what I saw the other night at Chatz you couldn't get enough of the guy. When he was talking, you leaned in and actually listened. Then, when I was leaving with Ben you were all over him. That's something."

"Maybe." She blushes. *Hey that's my bit...*

"So, let him know how you feel." I say as-matter-of-factly.

Erin stares at me blankly. "Says the one who won't open up to Ben?"

"Hey! I told him how I felt."

"Yeah, but really Tess? He didn't know you then. He took the time and consideration to make sure his father saw you. To make sure you had the best care he knew possible."

Damn. I effed up.

Chapter Twenty-One

Tess

I get Dave to cover for the rest of my week. I can't even imagine trying to make coffee and work a register with one hand. I'd just get hurt. Dave was pretty cool about it. He was insistent on coming over after work, but I wasn't in the mood. He then hissed out "One day you'll let me in."

So I passed the time in my small apartment, leaving only to walk down the block to the deli for food and coffee. I slept, cranked my music and attempted to paint. I know the way I acted or reacted was not the best. I bet he has forgotten about me. I tried to forget all about Ben Mitchell.

Epic failure.

It seemed like every song on my iPod reminded me of him. On Wednesday while listening to Blink-182, I thought about how if things were a little different that he could have fell in love with the girl at the rock show… instead of carrying her bloody body to the emergency room.

James brought me lunch and I caught him up. He was still hurt that I didn't call him first. But by the end of his visit, he seemed OK. But I have a feeling he will be checking up on me a little more now. Great.

On Thursday while listening to Good Charlotte, I thought about the secret I had held in for all these years. How we all have our secrets and want to hide them away. So no one will know we are weak. And you know what? Good Charlotte really seems to feel me right now, so I am screaming the songs out. Yes, this is my kind of therapy. Some people pray… I rock out.

By Friday, I can barely talk from scream singing my lungs out. Today, it's Pink. God, this woman is a goddess! It's late and I dance around my apartment in my boy shorts and sports bra. The lyrics make me cry, asking for reasons. Any kind of reason whether big or small just offer me something. I know we had something special.

By the end of the song, I am broken. I feel Ben everywhere. In my headphones, my speakers, the smell of him on my couch, and on my body. My heart. I need this man; I can understand what he did, even though I still need to hear it. But I feel like we have a connection that most people don't have. I haven't had any pain medication for twenty-four hours. I need a drink and I need my best friend.

I call Erin.

She arrives twenty minutes later, bearing booze. A lot of booze, I see as I read labels: "Vodka, tequila, lime juice, cranberry juice and whiskey?"

"Damn straight! I didn't know what you were in the mood for and I know you like your rum and cokes but I think tonight calls for something a little different."

"Well, my friend, you have no idea how much I need to get hammered."

She laughs. "Well, let's see, when we met you were a virgin. I have to ask; have you ever been drunk?"

I shake my head. And she hops around the room in a laughing fit. "So in a way I am busting your drunken cherry tonight?"

I laugh and give her a giant hug. "Aw, hey, what's wrong? No crying or getting all emotional UNTIL your drunk."

"Get to pouring, my friend," I tell her. And she eagerly gets to work on my first margarita...ever.

"So what do you think?" she asks after I take my first sip.

I scrunch my face with the burn of the tequila. "I like it. Bartender, I'll have another!" I say as I slam my glass down on the counter.

Erin smiles devilishly. "No. You, my girl, are taking a shot."

She pours tequila into a little glass. "Just toss it back, don't let it linger in your mouth and just swallow...but I am sure you know how to do that by now." She winks at me.

I pick up a spoon and throw it at her. "So not funny, Erin!" but I can't keep a serious face right now, and I think about Ben. Shit. This is why I wanted to get drunk. Here goes the shot. I do what I am told and it freaking burns!

I rasp out, seeking a clean breath. "How do people do these things one right after the other?" I ask Erin.

She shrugs. "Guess after the first couple, your mouth goes numb, that or you're too drunk to feel anything." Makes sense.

"In that case, give me another."

She does as she's told. "So, why the need to get drunk? Boy troubles? Is that why I am here instead of him?"

I slam back the second shot.

Gripping the counter with my one good hand, letting the gold liquid make its way down to my stomach, when I finally answer I can feel the alcohol hitting my head. "You could say that."

My lips unzip and I pour my guts out and tell Erin everything. By the time I am done we are on the red sofa and I have had three shots of tequila, and I'm working on a strong vodka cranberry.

Erin doesn't interrupt, but lets me get it out. When I am finally done she puts her two cents in. "I don't blame you for being angry with him. He saves you years ago and leaves you, but you didn't know each other then. Him, walking out on you a second time in the hospital after the time you spent together, is fucked up.

"He needs to get his shit together and make his choice, and if that choice is to stay away, then he needs to stay away forever. You don't need this crap, Tess. Oh! Can I got kick him in the balls or tip his bike and slash the tires?"

I love drunken Erin. I can't help but laugh; she has got me so drunk I can't stop laughing. This is what I needed, to let loose and laugh. We nearly finish the tequila and half of the contents in the vodka bottle.

We lay on my bed, talking about hot celebrity guys, and flat out pass out.

I wake up with what I am going to believe what is a hangover. I will never, ever pick on someone who has a hangover ever again. Erin is still passed out beside me. I decide to cover my head and go back to sleep.

Next thing I know, it's nearly two in the afternoon. Erin jumps up out of my bed. "Shit! I am going to be late to work at the restaurant! Shit! Shit! My boss said that if I am late one more time or show up drunk again he is going to fire my sorry ass."

"What time do you need to be at work?" I look at my clock.

She throws on her shoes and grabs her jacket. "Like thirty minutes ago. I am sorry to just run out on you like this,

Tess, but I need this job. I will call and check on you later, OK?"

"Yeah, I am fine. Go on, don't get fired!" I yell as she closes the door behind her. Now what?

Then it hits me. I texted Ben. I DRUNK texted Ben.

Oh no.

Coming back to me I fuzzily remember, Erin cheering me on, I remember her telling me to request a booty call. I don't know what I am going to say, but I feel the need to say something. So I log back into the Chatz chat room.

What did I say? I go on a mad dash for my phone. Opening up to the chat room I read:

Punky_Painter: "*Ben*"

That's all I seem to type out and he didn't reply. I think I am going to be sick.

Back to bed and to never come back out.

Chapter Twenty-Two

~ Ben ~

It's been nearly a week, and I have managed to keep my distance from Tess. I think it's for the best, considering how much of a letdown I am. Yeah, mum would be so proud of her son...

Then she texted me late last night, I wanted to call her. I wanted to go right over there and tell her how wrong she is and what she means to me. But I also think she needs time to heal and figure out things for herself. I just hope I have the self-restraint to let her...

The night of the Maroon 5 concert was the most amazing night of my life. I have had sex with a lot of women, I'll admit that, but none have been in my home, and none were remotely like Tess. I feel like an asshole for letting her trust me and to take something as special and private as her virginity, only to walk away. I did nothing but reinforce her doubts and fears. When I tried to contact her, she never replied. Then she texted me late last night, I wanted to call her. I wanted to go right over there and tell her how wrong she is and what she means to me. But I also think she needs time to heal and figure out things for herself. I just hope I have the self-restraint to let her...

Well, I did manage to get her photos off her camera that night while she was sleeping. Adam did say that he wanted to see them, so I e-mailed them to him directly and while I was at it, because they were amazing, truly amazing—even without any editing—I e-mailed them to the photo department at the magazine. She deserves to have her dream, even if I don't get to have mine with her. I also kept a copy of the photo we had taken with her. And I with the band...I just cropped those wankers out.

Chapter Twenty-Three

Tess

It's been one week since the second worst day of my life, but then maybe it was the worst, because I had feelings for my hero when he chose to leave that time. And to add insult to injury, my mom set up my follow-up appointment with Dr. Mitchell without telling me. So I am heading back the hospital. Oh, joy.

My mom begged to go with me, but I insisted that I was fine and wanted to just go in and get it over with. That, and I didn't want her in on the drama. I don't know if Dr. Mitchell will bring anything up about Ben, or keep it professional. I'm hoping for the latter.

My hand doesn't hurt as bad as it did a week ago, so that's a plus. But everything else hurts. Men like Ben don't change. He got what he wanted and he got out. I am hoping the doctor isn't in, or is on call at an emergency.

I pick at my cast and look around the soft blue room. The chairs are deep cherry wood with dark gray cushions. There's a waterfall cascading down a stone wall, which I am guessing are to calm me...Yeah, right that's so not going to happen.

The door next to the receptionist window opens and my name is called. A moment later, I'm in an exam room. It has the customary exam table, a table I never wanted to lay on again, not after the sort of exam I had to endure three years ago.

After that night, when the same doctor I am about to see now had reset my arm and bandaged my face, he suggested I get an internal exam because I was knocked unconscious and had no memory of what happened. So I agreed. I wanted to make sure that dick didn't get what he was so aggressively trying to take from me.

The nurse in front of me right now took my height, weight and blood pressure and my temperature. "Dr. Mitchell will be in a minute to see you, Ms. Martin."

Great, so he is here. What, no other young women saved by your amazing son? What a shame. Shit, what am I going to say if he brings up what happened? Does he know about everything? Does he know about me and Ben? I need to calm down before I have a panic attack. Just as I practice my calm breathing, I hear a light knock on the door.

"Hi, Tess, how are you?" He takes my right hand in a shake.

I return the gesture, with slight hesitation. His accent is just so familiar and I can now see and here where Ben gets it all from. "Hi, I am doing much better. My hand barely hurts, ready to get this bandaging off for good."

A moment later, I'm on the exam table He starts to cut my bandaging, but notices me cringing.

"Are you all right? Am I hurting you?" His voice is kind. It reminds me of how caring and compassionate Ben was our first night together...

"Uh, yeah, just didn't turn out so well the last time I had a sharp tool near my hand."

He laughs lightly and his smile truly reaches his eyes.

"So how bad of a scar are we talking about?" I ask.

Taking my hand to start cutting the threads, he begins. "Not too bad, my dear. Once these little buggers are out, you will start to see improvement shortly." Feeling relieved, I take in a deep cleansing breath. I just wish he could stitch up my heart.

"You and my son, are you dating? I know it's not exactly my place to ask..." I hold up my right hand to stop him.

"No, it's OK, I don't mind. Honestly I don't know what's going on with me and Ben."

He shows a small smile. "If you don't mind me saying, Tess, my son doesn't really 'date' as much as he 'entertains'. You seem like a very lovely and smart young woman, a young lady who would be good for my son. But I know how he goes through women, and I don't want to see that for you."

Wow. I have never met a father so honest about their own child, so honest and caring about someone else's child. I really like Jack. Ben is lucky to have such an awesome dad. "Thank you, Jack," I say. "I thought me and Ben had something, until we discovered that we knew one another in the not-so-pleasant past. When he brought me into the hospital that night, I didn't know who he was, I never saw a face. But it hurt me so bad to know that someone could just drop a beaten-up girl at the ER and just leave." I admit to him. I kind of hope he can voice some wise wisdom.

"My son, he had a tough adolescence. In London, he was expelled from three different schools for fights and a rotten attitude. He took the death of his mother very difficult; he was good at home and loved his baby sister, but outside he was a different person. He was shut off.

"When I was offered the job here and we moved to the States, I don't know... He just changed. He found his best mate and started a band. It was better than any therapy that he had ever received. Then he met Nicole in his senior year of high school, they were a good couple, even decided to go to college together. He was crazy about her and graduating college. And she cheats on him."

I nod, knowing parts of his story. "I know about Nicole and how they were supposed to get married. He also expressed his love for his mother and Caroline."

A warm smile spreads on his well-defined face. "Thank you, Tess. Just so you know, he doesn't tell anyone about his past or his family, he must have seen something special in you."

"Well, Jack, I see something special in him." And that's the last we speak of it. He finishes removing my stitches. It wasn't the most pleasant thing I have recently endured. But I'm happy to have them out.

It's still early and I have yet another day off work. I have enjoyed my time off to just paint, read and listen to music. I guess I became a hermit this week, but I enjoyed the company of my many book boyfriends. I feel pretty good so I just might try and go to my art class tonight. Depending on what we are doing, I might be able to participate.

I take a little nap before my evening class, but wake up an hour later hot and horny. This is new. I just woke up sweating and panting; even my panties are wet! Why am I like this? Oh. My dream.

Ben is in a band on stage. He is playing the bass and doing vocals, something you don't see much of; either it's the vocals alone or vocals and guitar. I am in the front row of a crowded bar room and there he is: tall, lean, muscles bulging in all the right spots. He's wearing nothing. Just his black and silver bass guitar, which is strategically covering his man parts. I feel like panicking. I don't want these other women to see him naked. He is for my eyes only. He is mine.

The other members of the band are fully clothed. Why is Ben the only naked one on the stage? He needs to get dressed; they can't see him. They start to play, his bass thumping, and I can feel its vibrations run up my calves, to my thighs and so on. Oh. He stares at me when he starts to sing, and his voice just about makes me come apart. I can't take my eyes off him. I know there are people all around me; they are starting to bounce around as the song begins to pick up pace. But I don't look at them. I keep my focus on the naked sex rock god in front of me on stage.

He stops singing actual lyrics and starts making moaning noises: the noises he made when we were making love. I don't want other people to hear those sounds. It's not right, it's private. He looks at me as he moans louder and he can tell I am upset. He looks to his right and left, to the other guys on stage with him, and nods for them to get lost. Now I am confused. He keeps strumming his bass, even though the rest of the band has left. He gives me his full panty-dropping smile when I nods in my direction. I look behind me to see what's going on and no one is in the room.

We are alone.

I cover my mouth in shock and appreciation, knowing now that no other women can see Ben. He is still strumming when he steps down off of the stage. Still strumming when he stops right in front of me, close enough to feel his hot sweet breath. I start to pant; I want this man more than anything I have ever wanted in my entire life. I reach out to stop his fingers from gliding up and down the neck of the bass. I place my hand on the neck of the bass. I slowly and teasingly start to stroke it from top to bottom, his gaze never leaving mine. He licks his lips; obviously he is affected by my movement. I use my other hand to pick the strings of the bass, a slow and seductive beat, gradually increasing pace, just like my breathing.

When I look down, I am naked. Well, isn't that convenient? He takes the pick in his right hand and runs it from the tip of my chin, down my neck, over my chest and between my breasts. It gives me chills. I let go of his bass and lift the strap over his shoulder, removing the instrument from his body, revealing his amazing form. Dropping to his knees before me, he reaches for my left foot and lifts it slowly, allowing me to balance myself. He takes the pick and runs it from my heel, up my arch and to the tip of my big toe. This causes me to convulse, and the feeling strikes me between the thighs. Placing my foot back down, he does the same to my left foot.

He stands and walks back to the stage. I follow him and once he reaches the edge of the stage, he turns and stops. I put my hand on his chest and force him to sit on the edge of the stage. Sitting, he leans back and rests on his elbows, as if waiting for something. I straddle him and slowly lower myself onto his incredible length. His eyes widen in what I assume is surprise; I am shocked at myself for taking the lead. I don't move once I take him into me fully; I want to savor the amazing fullness of him. He doesn't move. I think he wants me to take control; and I want to. I want to take this man, and do whatever I want to please me. I start to lift slowly on my knees and until he almost comes out completely, then I slam back down on him. He groans loudly and holds my hips as he reclines all the way back until he is flat on his back.

Neither of us speaks. We are just two hot bodies and harsh breaths. He doesn't take his gaze off of me. I feel powerful and confident. I have never felt that way about my body or my sexual abilities. He doesn't seem to be complaining. I pick up my speed as he grips my hips hard. His touch just makes me want more.

Faster and harder, I ride him. Still no words. He sits up and grabs me around my waist; now we are sitting face to face. He holds the back of my head and starts to grind his hips to mine. I am on the verge of an explosive climax. And then the silent treatment ends.

"I love you, Tess."

And I wake up.

Chapter Twenty-Four

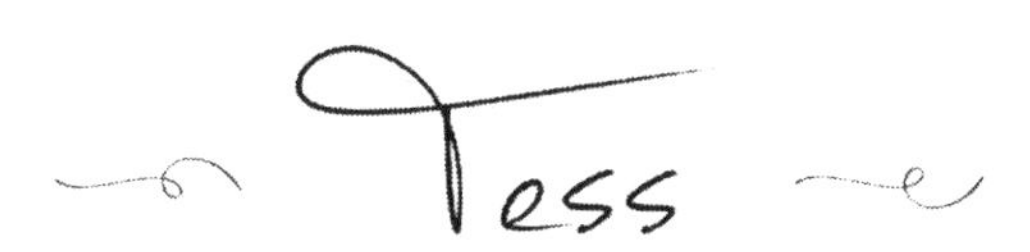

When I finally decide to crawl out of my bed late in the afternoon, I get a buzz on my intercom.

"Yeah?" I answer the buzz.

"Delivery for Miss Martin." I hear a young male's voice.

Thinking, I didn't order anything, hell I am going to have to ask my mom or James to help me out with rent this month. With all the lost time at work this past week. I don't like asking for help.

I tell him to come on up. When he reaches the door I am greeted with the largest most exquisite bouquet of pink peonies. I take them and the young man tells me to have a good day. I take my flowers back in and I notice a little blue envelope poking out, it reads: *Punky.*

I open the pale blue paper and pull out a photograph.

Oh. Oh, I am going to cry.

It's the photo from the concert, but it's just of me and Ben. I know I have the original picture, but how did he get this? We both look happy. I turn over the photo to see a message from Ben:

Tess,

If I could offer you a reason, any reason at all for what happened I would. I don't know how we went from what we were to nothing at all. I understand your hurt over what happened three years ago, but I was a different person then. I have changed considerably. You have changed me. I can only hope that one day you can forgive me, because I will never forgive myself for losing you.

You have my heart. Forever.

Ben

There is no way I can focus, and we now know what happens when I get distracted in art class... I don't want to face Ms. S just yet, not while she knows I was/am seeing her own boyfriend's son. How and when did this involve so many people? And besides I can't seem to find my sketchbook anywhere. *Man, if I left it at Ben's...*

I call Dave and see if the coffee shop needs an extra hand tonight. I need to occupy myself any way I can. If I don't I will go running to Ben and as much as I want to, I don't know what I would say.

"I am actually not working tonight, so I was planning on hitting up a club. Why don't you tag along with me?" I do need to get out, clear my head. Why not have a few drinks with my co-worker? It's not like he's asking me out on a date.

"Sure, why not," I say.

I can practically hear him smile. "Oh, this will be fun, baby doll! Why don't you meet me at Pearl at ten tonight."

I laugh at the nickname he gave me when we started working together two years ago. I can't believe we have never hung out. Now that I think about it, it's not like he hasn't tried. He often asked what I was doing after a shift, but I always told him I am not one to go out and party. I'm still not, but tonight I need to forget about Ben for a couple of hours. It's bad enough that he's invading my dreams now.

"Sounds great, Dave, see you then."

Now what to do with the rest of the day...

I grab my camera and head for Pike Place Market. I need some fresh fruit and that's the place to go. I love the feeling of the place, so real and full of life. You never know what you're going to find or see.

I snap shots of the rows of colorful produce, and of a young boy no older than three biting into an apple bigger than his hands. His eyes are wide with surprise; it's a perfect shot and it makes me giggle. The air is cool and crisp and feels amazing in my lungs. I just wander the market picking up apples, strawberries; eggplant, zucchini and bananas...*damn bananas the shit heads remind me of Ben's first visit to my place.*

Later, back home, I Google Pearl. It's not a gay club, but a swanky upbeat club that features up and coming DJs. Well, this should be interesting; I just hope it's not rap music, I just can't stand that stuff...bitches and hos just isn't my thing I guess... I decide on my black fake leather pants and a white tank top with my black studded leather jacket and my over-the-knee black boots. I refuse to be the kind of girl who shows up wearing a shiny tube top and mini skirt. I mean, that's what they wear in the movies, right?

At the club, I hear Dave call my name from the door.

He offers me an arm, like a gentleman, and leads me into the large space. We look down to the dance floor. Music thumps and lights shoot everywhere. Dave walks me around to one of the many bar areas.

"Swanky," I say.

Dave laughs and orders us drinks.

The blonde pinup delivers our drinks and gives Dave a wink. ha! If she only knew he was gay... I reach for my drink and take a sip through the small straw, without asking what it was. It's fruity and strong! Holy shit, is it strong!

I nearly spit it out. "What is this?" I ask.

"It's called a Zombie."

"I do like rum, but this"—I hold up my glass—"is insane."

We chat about his recent love life, which apparently isn't going so well. And of course he asks me about mine.

"I have sort of been seeing this one guy, but it's complicated. I don't think we are going to be seeing each other again." I want to leave it at that.

He sets his empty glass down, stands up and holds out his hand. I take it and he leads me to a wide set of stairs. Once at the bottom I see that the whole bottom floor is a dance floor. Crap.

"I can't dance!" I yell into Dave's ear.

"Of course you can, baby doll. Just loosen those hips and sway to the beat."

I roll my eyes, cringe and start to move.

The dance floor becomes more crowded once a new DJ takes on the turntables. The beat is decent and the booze is really hitting me. I needed this tonight, to just relax and let loose. Maybe I should come out with Dave a little more often and bring Erin along.

Erin's been pretty busy this past week with her "flavor of the week," as she puts it, but I think it's more than that. I could see some sort of connection when she was making out with that Mark guy at Chatz last week. So I haven't seen much of her since.

A couple of guys try to dance with me, but I shrug them off. I am flattered but I don't want to dance with a guy who is probably just looking for a lay. Then I come up with a brilliant plan. "Hey Dave!" I yell into his ear. "Wanna be my boyfriend tonight?"

His eyebrows shoot up. "Um, sweetie...I don't swing that way. Thought you knew that." He winks.

I roll my eyes and smile. "No, I know that! It's just I am tired of these guys trying to bump and grind on me tonight. Can you just pretend to be my boyfriend? Dance a little closer so they can take a hint?" Even after I say it, it sounds ridiculous.

The good friend he is, he moves in a lot closer behind me. "How's this? Will the guys back off if they see us like this?" My heart starts to race. I feel crowded, something isn't right. I need to get away. I need to text Ben. I feel like I am about to die. I can't breathe.

I shove away from Dave and I head to the ladies room, on the opposite side of the dance floor and down a long red hallway with numerous doors. On my way I text Ben: *"At Pearl, come get me. I need you."*

God, I hope I can make it... The ladies room is at the end. One of the doors open and I stumble inside.

I fall to the floor with a thud. "What the hell?" I say out loud. The lights are so dim, I can barely see anything, but it looks kind of like a storage room. No one speaks. Did I lean on the door and fall in? How much did I have to drink?

I hear the door slam shut. I definitely did not fall in.

I hear footsteps come at me. My pulse races. I try to get up but I can't move...What the fuck? I feel a set of hands on my knees. I try to jerk away but fail, and the hands move higher and higher.

"Who are you? Stop." I gasp out and it took all of my energy for the short few words and then it hits me: *I've been drugged.* I try to scream but it only comes out an airy silence. My heart feels like it's about to explode, I am so scared. I don't know who this is or why they have me in here, but I have a pretty good idea when I feel hands running up my shirt.

This is all too familiar, I think as I smell and feel a warm breath at the side of my face.

Then the male voice speaks.

"I have been waiting for three years to finally finish what I started that night at the concert."

And with those words I want to die. Just kill me. I don't want to live with this fear, or the aftereffects of what is about to happen to my body. I feel my pants being unbuttoned and being pulled down until they are completely off. Then I hear the terrifying words from a voice that used to make me smile.

"Oh, what I am going to do to you, baby doll." It's Dave. Dave is the man who violently punched me and backhanded me and tried to rape me.

It takes all of my strength to ask the one question that has been plaguing me for three years: "Why?"

"Why, you ask?" Dave spits out.

"It wasn't personal then. I didn't seek you out or anything. You're small and I figured you wouldn't be able to fight me off. I was drunk and high and I needed to fuck. I didn't give a shit what it did to the girl. I was fucking getting what I wanted until some fuck-ass beat the shit out of me, and I needed reconstructive surgery to my face.

"It wasn't personal until the cops came, and the security guard that saw the whole thing gave his statement. I didn't have to face jail time, because no one pressed charges...because no one tattletaled." He points at me with a creepy, terrifying grin.

"I was unrecognizable after my face was practically ripped off, and after having numerous plastic surgeries. I knew no one from that night would or could recognize me." He touches his face as he speaks.

"I was able, however, to sweet talk the receptionist at the hospital for my 'cousins' records from that night, to see who was brought in from a concert...I was able to find a name and a photo. So I tracked her down and just waited for my time for payback on the little bitch." He sounds so turned off. No emotion. His body is relaxed, which is confusing, given the circumstances.

"So, when I saw that she was working in a small café, I figured why not apply, become friends, gain trust, and really tear her apart. Oh, and what better way than to pretend to be gay? Girls these days just love to have a gay guy friend." He winks and does the stereotypical limp wrist.

"Now, I am going to get what I want after all this time." He reaches into his back pocket and unfolds a piece of paper.

Throwing in my face, I then see what it is. My sketch of Ben's face, from class. The sketch that was in my missing sketchbook. Why does he have this? How? Oh my God, he's the one who got into my apartment.

Dropping it to the floor, "And now your boyfriend is going to pay..."

And then he's on me, too fast for my drugged body to react. I want to scream, my throat burns too badly. Just as his hands are around the sides of my underwear, the door slams open.

"Tess?" an English accent roars through the small room. The lights go on. Dave stands and launches himself at Ben, but he's too slow, and Ben punches him square in the face. Dave recovers quickly, and slams his right fist into Ben's stomach, but Ben doesn't seem to be fazed. Ben swiftly throws Dave to the floor and kicks him in the ribs. I hear a violent crack that turns my stomach. I know all too well what that feels like...

I see Ben hover over Dave and throws punch after punch into his face and his sides. When Dave goes limp, Ben stands and rushes to me.

"Tess, are you all right?" He looks me over.

"Did he fucking touch you?" His jaw is clenched.

"No," I manage to squeak out.

His face contorts. "What did he do, then? You have to tell me, Tess, right now or I am going to kill this guy and go to jail."

"Drugged" I say in a breath, looking him in the eyes. I am so scared.

His dark eyes widen and he scoops me up into his arms. "We have to get you to the hospital, Tess." I don't want to go, but I don't know what Dave put in my drink and I don't want to die, not while I have Ben with me. I have missed him so much. A tear runs down my cheek and he notices.

"It's going to be OK, baby, I promise." For once, I feel like it is.

He leads me to his car, sets me up in the front seat, and calls 911. Then he races to the ER.

Chapter Twenty-Five

~ Ben ~

It's been an hour since they took her back. Dad's not in tonight, so I can't ask him what's going on. Fuck! If I could have just manned up and faced what had happened front-on, we never would have stopped seeing one another this past week. She never would have gone out to that club. I am just fucking relieved that I was there covering the new DJ for the magazine.

I thought I saw Tess on the dance floor with a guy, but I didn't think it was my place to step in. It looked like she was having a good time. When I saw her walk to the hall with the bathrooms, when she texted me. I saw her date, or whoever, walk after her, then run behind one of the small bar areas and through a door. She said she needed me in her text. Fuck, something was really wrong. I started going through every door in that hall.

The minute I saw her, I lost it. I didn't care if she was consenting to the guy or not, she was mine. She *is* mine. No other man can have her like I have. But her text...that's what worried me. She needed me.

So I jumped the guy. I didn't care who he was.

Now I am stuck waiting. This is what I should have done that very first night. Waited.

Finally a nurse comes out and asks if I am with Tess. She takes me back to a small room. I rush in and I see her little body hooked up to IVs and machines.

"Is she OK?" I ask the nurse.

She checks Tess's blood pressure. "The doctor will be in shortly to discuss it with you." She walks out.

I walk over to Tess and I take the hand that's free of IV lines. I lift it to my mouth to kiss it. It's too much. I drop to my knees and I cry. I haven't cried since my mother passed away. I don't know what to do to make this up to her. I need her, I can't lose her.

A knock on the door startles me. "Hi, you must be with Tess," a doctor says as he enters the room.

"Yes. I am her boyfriend. Is she going to be all right? What's going on?"

"She is going to be fine. She is sleeping now, because we found a fair amount of the drug Rohypnol—in other words, roofies—in her system. That is why she was unable to speak or move when you brought her in. We have her on fluids and are monitoring her heart rate."

"When will she wake up?" I ask.

"The drug will be in her system for a little while longer. That is why we are keeping her well hydrated, hoping to flush it out of her system faster."

I nod. "Thank you."

The doctor forces a smile. "If you have any questions, feel free to have one of the nurses page me." He turns to leave.

I return to Tess, pulling a chair up to the bed. I hold her hand to my cheek and wait for her to wake up.

I must have dozed off, because when I wake up three hours have passed and Tess is still asleep. I stand to stretch out my back; I had fallen asleep hunched over the side of the bed, with my head on her lap. I walk over to the window and stretch out, and as I do, I hear movement from the bed. I turn to see Tess moving her arms and legs. Thank god.

I rush back to her side. "Tess, it's OK. You're in the hospital. I am here."

She licks her lips; they're probably dry. "Ben?."

"Yes, baby, I am here." I grab her hand and kiss it. A small smile crosses her face.

"You saved me again." Her eyes flutter open to look at me.

I lose it. I start to sob. I can't help it any longer, I thought I had lost her before, but this was far worse. She could have been killed.

"I am so sorry, Tess. I shouldn't have acted like a jerk. I should have stayed by you. I am so sorry." I try to stop my crying as I speak.

She takes in a slow deep breath. "I know. I'm not mad or upset. I can't be, not with you."

I lean over her and kiss her on the cheek.

"Is that all you got, Bond?" I laugh through my last tears. I grab her face with both of my hands and kiss her. Hard.

A knock on the door disturbs out moment. Damn it. It's a police officer. "Sorry to interrupt, but I need Ms. Martin's statement now."

Tess blushes a little and nods. The officer asks for the name of Tess's attacker, and I hear it for the first time.

"How do you know Mr. Stratton?"

"Initially we worked together for two years. But after tonight I learned that I knew him from three years ago."

Now I am confused.

"How is that, Ms. Martin?" the cops asks her.

She closes her eyes and looks up at me. "Dave was the one who tried to attack me at a concert three years ago. Ben here saved me from him then, not knowing me at the time. He told me tonight that he had to have a lot of facial surgeries to fix what Ben did. And he wanted revenge. So he stalked me and befriended me into trusting him, so he could get his wish. He also broke into my apartment and stole my sketchbook. It had a detailed sketch of Ben in there and he threw it in my face, telling me that 'your boyfriend will pay'"

I am going to kill the fucker. I should have the first time.

The cop nods. "That's what Mr. Stratton admitted to as well this evening when we picked him up."

Smart move, asshole. You're lucky to be behind bars.

The officer says he'll take a full statement later, and leaves.

"I thought you said this Dave guy was gay?" I ask her.

She shrugs. "That's what he made me believe to raise the trust bar. Sick, right?"

"Very. Thankfully they have him now and I don't have any plans on letting you go," I tell her.

She smiles and takes my hand. "Good."

Epilogue

Tess

It's been four days since my attack. I recovered pretty quickly, and returned to work as normal on Wednesday. Ben has been busy with his new feature from covering the DJ from Pearl that night. Tonight, however, both of us are free.

I decide to pull out the dress Erin begged me to buy on our shopping trip. It's spaghetti-strapped, with a deep red corset-ribbed top, and the bottom part is black, with thin layers of sheer material. I pair it with my crimson red pumps that match my lipstick perfectly. I do a half pull back with my hair allowing my shorter strands to fall loose around my face. Looking in the mirror, I hardly recognize myself, but you know what? For the first time in my life I feel hot, and just might fit in with the in crowd at the bar tonight. Ben mentioned he might stop in for a drink at Chatz tonight. Apparently he and the burly bartender are friends.

I look around for Ben's Ducati, but thankfully I don't see it...yet. I know Chatz is going to be crawling with horny drunks looking for a hookup. God, I can see all the typos now on the screen...

The bar is full, but I spot an empty seat at the end. The same burly bartender asks for my ID again, even though he has seen me a couple of times now. He looks at my license and back to me, raising an eyebrow.

"You were here a couple of times the other week. Damn, you look different! Hot!" he exclaims. I give a polite smile. I have never taken compliments well; they make me feel uncomfortable.

"Rum and Coke, please."

I pull out my phone and get logged in. As soon as I enter the chat room, it's full of come-ons, bad pickup lines and drunken typos, just as I predicted.

I sit and watch the conversations.

Jeremy88: Hey *SweetSarah how you doin' baby?*

SweetSarah: *Hey Jeremy88 I am doing good, a little tipsy and ready for someone to take me home, why don't you give your hand a little raise so I know who I am going home with tonight.*

Wow, really? I don't think I have seen a woman be so forward here before. It's kinda cool and refreshing. Why shouldn't she just go for what she wants? I keep watching the screen when...oh shit.

Slippery_When_Wet69: *Hey Big_Ben I know your hiding in here somewhere, come out, come out wherever you are.*

Big_Ben: *I told you to leave me the fuck alone. I am not here for you or anyone else tonight.*

Whoa.

Slippery_When_Wet69: *Oh come on baby I will take care of you. You seem down, let me make it all better.*

I wait for Ben to say something to her, when I see a little red dot appear at the top of my screen
"1 Private Message"
Ben...oh thank God.

Big_Ben: *Tess what are you doing here? And where are you sitting? I don't see you.*

Punky_Painter: *I'm at the bar. I was hoping to see you.*

Big_Ben: *I'm not here looking for a hookup Tess. Please don't think. I just came in for a drink before I went home.*

Punky_Painter: *Come talk to me, please.*

Big_Ben: *Weren't you supposed to be working tonight?*

You know what? I have had enough if this softball crap. I get up and walk to the restroom. In a stall, I hang up my purse.

Big_Ben: *I am at the bar, where did you go?*

I tip the top of my dress and let my breasts peek out, and I hold out my phone and snap a photo. I can't believe I am actually doing this, but I want to get his attention somehow.

And I hit send.

I wait for a reply, but I don't get one. I hear someone come into the bathroom. And what sounds like the door being locked. What the hell?

I am the only one in here, so this doesn't make sense. I watch the floor and the space between the stall door and the floor, and I see a pair of nice black MEN'S dress shoes stop at my stall, and then hear a small knock. My heart is racing at this point. I am no longer someone who likes to be snuck up on. Not after everything that has happened. I am about to freak out and scream, I hear a very familiar accent "Tess."

When I open the stall, I see Ben. Oh, God he looks so hot and tasty in his suit. He looks at me with hooded eyes, and I realize my breasts are barely covered. I cover myself up as he enters the stall and closes the door.

My breathing hitches; I am wet already. He hasn't yet touched me and I am ready for him. He gently grabs my elbow to steer my back against the stall door and pins my body between his thick arms as they reach out on both sides of my head, trapping me.

I lick my red-stained bottom lip when he leans in closer. That's all it took. His mouth was on mine so fast I didn't have a chance to release my lip, but he did it for me. He thrusts his tongue in my eager mouth. I need him, I need to taste him. I reach down for his belt, then his button, and finally his zipper.

Then I do something I have never done before. I drop to my knees. I reach into his pants; he is already hard as a rock. I stroke him for a moment and I look up at him. He stares at me as I lick the tip of his head and a tight gasp escapes his lips, this giving me the courage to take him deep into my mouth and as far as I could in my throat. He groans loudly and holds my head. I pick up my pace, sucking and licking every long delicious inch of him. He rocks his hips with my rhythm, and as soon as I am about to go deep again, he pulls away. Backing up enough to look me in the eyes, he puts his index finger under my chin and urges me to stand up. I do.

His mouth goes for my breasts, fully exposed now, and he sucks and teases one nipple and rolling the other with his thumb and forefinger. I throw my head back and moan. He moves his eager mouth to my neck and hikes up the hem of my dress. I feel him rip off my lace thong. Holy crap, that is incredibly hot. He reaches up my thigh and slips his fingers between my lips and begins to tease me. Not being able to take any more, I break the silence.

"Fuck me." I tell him.

"No."

"Why? I need you."

He looks me in the eye. "I told you once already, Tess. I won't fuck you. You are more than a fuck or a lay. What I am going to do to you is press you up against this stall door and make love to you fast and very hard."

I nearly come at his words. "Then do it, make love to me. But you can't leave me anymore. You have done it one too many times now, in the times I have needed you the most. Even when I didn't know it was you that night, I needed YOU."

"I know." He takes a condom out of his pocket, tears it open with his teeth and rolls it on. He lifts me at my waist, pushing my back against the door, and I feel the head of his dick at my opening.

"Please," I beg with a whimper, and he slams into me just as he promised, hard and fast. I let out a high-pitched squeal and catch a smile on his lips. He keeps up his fast pace and as I feel myself building, going higher and higher, he moans my name, and I am lost. I am soaring above Earth, searching for my body, as I come plummeting back.

We are both breathing heavily when he carefully lowers me to the floor and helps fix the straps to my dress. He then pinches the tip of the condom, squinting as he pulls it off and tosses it in the toilet behind him.

"I really hate these suckers," he says with a little snicker.

I giggle a little. "I can see about going on the pill. That is, if we are going to make this a regular thing."

He smirks. "Oh, it will be. If you'll have me?"

"Sir, are you asking to be mine?" I tease him in a mock English accent.

He raises an eyebrow. "Well, whenever I asked you to be mine, you never fully answered so I may as well ask to be yours."

I lick my lips and nod slowly.

"Let me buy you a drink." he states.

We walk out of the restroom to find a line of women impatiently waiting.

Oh, crap, crap! People know that we just had a quickie in a public restroom. I probably look like a pretty big slut right now. Then Ben does something that surprises me: He takes my hand. And leads me down the slim hallway back out to the bar. I look to the right and to the left to see the women glaring at me, passing their judgments on me. Then one speaks up. "I see how it is, Ben, you take the short dog into the toilet for a quick screw but you won't even give me the time of day?"

Ben stops in his tracks and turns toward her. "If you EVER say anything like that again to or about my GIRLFRIEND, I will be sure that everyone will know what you did to Dan and what kind of a dirty bag you are. Do you understand me, Jackie?"

I look up; she has the look of pure horror and humiliation. Good. Jackie just nods. I wonder how he knows her or her name and what dirt he has on her.

Ben offers me a stool at the bar and sits next to me, not letting go of my hand.

"Girlfriend, huh?" I ask him.

He smiles his million-dollar panty-dropping smile. "Is that all right with you? I know you wanted to know last week what we were. I suppose now I know and so do you."

I try to resist the megawatt smile from spreading across my face. "What makes you think I want to be your girlfriend?"

He leans in close to my ear, brushing his lips against my cheek and says, "Because what you and I have is the most important thing to me and I will not let you slip through my fingers, that and you're not the 'fuck 'em and leave 'em' kind of girl."

I am literally panting.

I sigh. "I guess you're right, Bond. You have officially ruined me."

He lightly laughs. "Back to Bond, are we? Punky?"

The sound of our nicknames makes me full on laugh and snort a little. Oh God! I cover my face in horror, but Ben pulls them away and holds them both.

"Don't ever hide who you are."

I blush. "So who was that woman and what did she do to Dan?" I ask him

"Let's get our drinks, head to a sofa, and I will tell you." He orders us glasses of moscato. We sit; he puts his long arm around my shoulder. Oh, I am loving this. He is so warm and smells a mix of me and him. I take a little sip of my wine and notice him staring at my mouth.

I put my free hand on his thigh. "So...?"

"All right, so, when my family and I moved here from London, Dan was a guy who lived up the street and we became fast friends, and even attempted a little band out of his garage. We were inseparable. He's a great guy and even though we didn't go to the same college, we ended up working at *Tones* together. We have been friends since we were fifteen."

He pauses, takes a sip of his wine, licks his tasty lips, and I oh so bravely push myself up and lick them myself. I have no self-control at the time being. He looks at me with burning eyes when I settle back down next to him.

"Like I was saying...Dan and I worked at Tones together and he started to date this girl, who he fell pretty hard for. They dated for nearly a year, and one day he discovers he has crabs. Now we all know you can get crabs from a public toilet, but in Dan's case it was because his girlfriend was cheating on him with any guy who would look at her, and that was a lot."

"Jackie?"

He nods his head. "Yes. So obviously Dan dumped her ass, before he could catch another STD, and was so humiliated and fed up that he asked to be relocated to another location."

"So do you still see Dan?" I can tell he misses his old friend.

"Here and there, when he has to come back for a major meeting, but that's not too often. We do stay in touch on Facebook and text one another."

I have a thought. "The first time I came here and was watching all the conversations, I saw a girl being very persistent with you in the chat room. You said something like 'not after what you did' and you told her to get lost. Was that Jackie? Is Jackie Slippery_When_Wet69?"

He lets out a deep grumble that I can feel in my thighs. "Yeah, she keeps trying to get with me, because I am the only one who's never came onto her."

"I understand that. Wanting something that you can't have it totally sucks. So do I have anything to worry about?" The way I say it, I hope he hears it like '*do I have to worry about you sleeping with the slut or anyone else for that matter?*'

He looks me right in the eye. Leans in, and presses his forehead to mine, and says, "No."

"So, what now?" I ask him.

He gives me a sly smile. "Don't be mad. But that night after the Maroon 5 concert...while you were sleeping I e-mailed your photos to the band like Adam asked, and to my boss."

Oh. OH?

"My boss would like to meet with you about a possible job offer. One that requires you to photograph the shows I attend."

"Oh. My. God!" is all that comes out.

I attack him with a body-crushing kiss.

My twisted knight in dark shiny armor.

Acknowledgements

First I would like to thank my husband, for putting up with my hours and obsessing about this book, going after the boys when I was typing away and not committing me to the insane asylum for when I talked about my characters as if they were real people.

Thank you mom, you were so supportive over this and along with everything I do, but took in everything I had to say and let me vent. Don't look at me when you read it! Yes a little awkward haha.

Especially for my best friend Katie Potvin! You my dear have put up with so much of my book talk that you deserve a medal! I have loved gushing over the detail with you. And to my friend from afar bestie Heather Putnam, for being the first to read my extremely raw first draft and for cheering me on, I love you so much for putting up with me.

To the amazing author Jenn Sterling, whose book inspired me to "prove it" and pursue my dreams. Also to new author friend Jessica Park for being stunning! Giving me tips and even putting me in contact with her and now my editor.

Thank you for all your "tough love" Jim Thomsen, my amazingly cool editor! You bared though my rough manuscript and have taught me so much. You are more than a copy-editor; you are a teacher and a great person. Thank you for all the help you have offered me.

To all my girls on InstaGram and the members of SMI Bookclub, who were the first to know about this book. You all have shown me more love than I knew possible, I wish I could hug each and every one of you.

My beta readers:, Christy D., Claudia C., Elise T., Jade G., Michelle F., Candace C., Stephanie O., Tasha T., you are all my lovies!

To my best friend's hubby and my friend Randy Potvin, for helping me clean up my manuscript and designing my cover with me! You are multi-talented and can go far with your gifts.

Joe Marvullo. What can I say? I made a little comment on one photo on your IG, not expecting any sort of reply back and you offer yourself to me. You showed me something that I have never seen in person before, unconditioned kindness. I have heard people talk about it, but never witnessed it for myself. I am grateful and extremely thankful, I cannot express this enough. So thank you.

Joe Marvullo's Links

Model Mayhem: www.modelmayhem.com/jmarvullo

Facebook: https://www.facebook.com/joe.marvullo.1?fref=ts

Sam Roman, thank you so much for posing with Joe on this cover. You are very beautiful and I couldn't have imagined anyone better.

Photographer David Massa, thank you for helping make my cover dreams come true.

Thank you Randy Potvin for putting my cover together for me! You brought my vision to life! You are extremely talented and I couldn't be happier with my cover!

Author Links

I love to connect with readers! Get in touch with me and let me know what you thought of *Private Message.*

Facebook author page:
https://www.facebook.com/pages/Author-Danielle-Torella/396408743800429?ref=hl

Facebook personal page:
https://www.facebook.com/danielle.torella

Blog:
http://authordanielletorella.blogspot.com/

Goodreads:
http://www.goodreads.com/author/show/7059361.Danielle_Torella

Made in the USA
Charleston, SC
20 June 2013